TIME STRANGER

Time Travel Romance

by

Elyse Douglas

COPYRIGHT

"People like us, who believe in physics, know that the distinction between past, present and future is only a stubbornly persistent illusion."

—Albert Einstein

For Kathy

TIME STRANGER

PART 1

CHAPTER 1
London 1944

Anne Billings heard the eerie whine of air raid sirens and the deep-throated drone of German bombers approaching from the east. Her eyes turned skyward, seeing the barrage balloons floating lazily in the sky to discourage low-level attacks. But these bombers were not flying at a low level. They were flying high, above ten thousand feet.

A sickening fear seized her stomach, and she grasped four-year-old Tommy's little hand so tightly that he cried out, "Mummy, that hurts!"

"Come on, Tommy, hurry, we have to run for it. We have to get to the shelter."

As she yanked him across the street, Tommy tilted his head back, his wide eyes viewing the mass of bombers filling the sky. He pointed, scared, on the verge of tears. "Are those airplanes going to drop bombs, Mummy?"

The streets filled with panic as scattering crowds ran for the air raid shelter—struggling old men with canes; elderly women with stiff knees; mothers with babies cradled in their arms, their faces set in grim determination.

An air raid warden blew his shrill whistle, frantically waving the streaming crowds toward the entrance of the shelter, only a block away.

"Step lively, now! Step lively!"

Above, the bombers burst through rusty clouds, visible now, the frightening drone of their engines filling Anne's ears, the bombs already screaming earthward.

Anne had been so close to seeing him. Just an underground ride away and they'd have met; she would have seen him and kissed him: First Lieutenant Kenneth Cassidy Taylor, her American sweetheart, Kenneth. They had planned to spend a wonderful day together, just the three of them—Tommy, Kenneth and her—a day she'd been looking forward to for so long.

The sharp autumn wind scattered dry leaves and whipped up the red in Tommy's cheeks as they hurried, breathless, almost at the shelter.

Bombs whistled down, roaring, bursting, the deafening sound rolling like thunder, splitting earth and sky asunder as if it were the end of the world.

A store to Anne's right was struck by a bomb, and brick, wood and burning bodies were blown all over the street. A hot blast of wind whooshed in like a great fist, nearly knocking Anne off her feet. She screamed, tugging a terrified Tommy away.

Wobbling on unsteady feet, she and Tommy stumbled on, as chaotic sparks rained down all around them.

Out of control, a jeep roared by, plunged across the street and swerved, just missing them. It slammed into a lamppost, horn blaring, as a string of bombs blew out the side of a building. Bricks went flying, smoke billowed, and a wall collapsed, burying a young couple who'd been running for the shelter.

A bright flash blinded Anne, and she threw up a hand to shade her eyes, squinting, disoriented and dizzy. She lost sight of the shelter. And then the horror seemed to unfold in slow motion. A bomb shattered a shop, glass flew, and in a whirlwind of heat and dust, Tommy was ripped from Anne's hand. Another blast hurled her into the air, her body floating, weightless. She seemed to sail, her arms reaching, her legs kicking, her mouth stretched in shock.

When she crashed to the pavement, the air burst from her lungs, and pain splintered her body. The stink of oil, blood and burning rubber assaulted her senses and, in her dazed stupor, she tried to reach, tried to speak—to call out for Tommy—but her diaphragm seized up in agonizing spasms. Her wild eyes searched, her mind a muddle, her body stunned by a knifing pain.

Houses toppled, angry red flames shot up into the blackened sky, and bricks lay scattered about the street near tattered furniture, twisted overturned autos, and broken bodies. A few feet away, a smoking crater was all that remained of where the air raid warden had stood, waving them to the shelter.

Someone staggered against a bombed-out building, face in their hands, the moaning sounds of death and destruction everywhere.

A bomb came raining down and smashed into a row of houses; windows exploded, lampposts were blown high and whirling, bicycles flung, and bodies tossed. Anne felt herself flying, flailing and dying.

In her head she screamed, "Tommy!"

CHAPTER 2
New York City 2008

Anne swam up from the depths of dark dreams, swatting away fleeing images and faces, hearing terror screams, feeling pain shoot through her body. Her eyes seemed glued together, and she strained to open them. Bright light crashed in and she quickly squeezed them shut, her world spinning, her breathing labored.

She shivered, heard voices and the wobbling cry of a siren. She felt hands touch her, and she struggled to push them away with arms that wouldn't move, with hands that twitched, with a body that convulsed.

Her mind screamed out panic and pain—such excruciating pain—that it finally engulfed her, and she dropped back into a dark ocean of sleep, where airplanes roared overhead, where bombs fell, and the smell of fear and death were all around her.

She awoke, lost and searching. Her vision wouldn't focus; every sound hurt, and she was strapped to the bed. There was the blur of movement and the echo of voices.

What were those tubes, drips and beeping monitors? When her eyes opened fully, she saw orange, and she burned like fire. Something pricked her arm, and she faded away into blackness, the welcome cover of blackness.

When she next awoke, she heard something odd and unfamiliar—an IV pump alarm. She heard people whispering; the rasping sound of an airplane flying overhead; and a laundry cart rattling down the hospital corridor.

Where was she? She was lying in a bed. Hospital? She was warm. Her head felt heavy and stuffed with cotton, her throat dry. Fatigue overwhelmed her again, and she dropped into a deep sleep.

She awakened to the pungent smell of hospital disinfectant, the wheezing sound of her breath, and the persistent beep, beeping sound of something irritating. Why didn't it stop?

She floated up from the depths of sleep to consciousness, and her eyes fluttered open. Her head was bandaged to the tops of her eyes; her right shoulder was in an elaborate sling, and she had a long tube inserted into her wrist.

An effort to move brought dull pain. Another try failed, as a drugged clumsiness kept her still and scared. She noticed that a privacy curtain was open just enough for her to see her room was dimly lit, with a window to her left revealing darkness beyond it.

Her eyes lifted to see a blank monitor perched up high and angled down, and she saw her own vague reflection in it. *What is that?* she thought. As she gradually awakened to nearly full consciousness, a sudden sense of fear and danger struck her in the gut. Where was she and what had happened to her? Her mind reeled; her pulse raced; breath came in quick pants of alarm.

When she heard whispers and muffled voices drawing close, she shut her eyes, hoping everything would vanish: the pain, the confusion and the stampeding fear.

A soft, male voice startled her, and she kept her eyes tightly shut.

"Are you awake?" the voice asked. "How are you feeling?"

She slowly cleared her throat, her breath coming fast through her nose.

"Just relax..." the soothing voice said. "You're going to be fine. Just fine."

Slowly, reluctantly, Anne opened her eyes, blinking several times to focus on the face above her.

"Hi there," he said, smiling.

She looked at him, squinting. It was a kind face; his smile was reassuring. His sandy hair was styled in an odd way, long in front, short on the sides, but the face was handsome and young; maybe he was in his late thirties.

Anne cleared her throat and tried to speak, but her voice was low and raspy, and she was unable to produce any audible words.

"You don't have to talk. It's okay. I'm your doctor, Dr. Miles, Dr. Jon Miles. I was making my rounds, and I wanted to see how you're feeling."

Anne forced a word out. "Where?"

"Do you mean, where are you?" Dr. Miles clarified. She nodded.

"You're at Lenox Hill Hospital."

Anne worked to understand. "Lenox...?"

"Yes. You were found in Central Park a little over a week ago and brought here by ambulance."

Dr. Miles saw the terror in Anne's eyes, and he sought to calm her. "You're doing amazingly well, Miss, Mrs.? I'm afraid we don't know your name. You had no identification on you when you were found by a jogger, and no one has come forward to identify you. What is your name?"

She stared blankly. "Name?"

"Yes... You were admitted anonymously. We will need to know who you are, where you live and what insurance you have. We also need to contact your next of kin."

"My name?" she repeated, a new fear surfacing.

Dr. Miles removed his hands from the white lab coat. "Yes... May I know your name?"

Anne blinked rapidly, her face pale. "Well... I ... I'm... Well, I'm not sure."

Dr. Miles couldn't hide his concern. "That's fine. You've been through a lot and you need more rest."

Anne felt the rise of a towering panic that heated her cheeks. "But... My name... I... should know that... shouldn't I?"

Her voice trailed off and tears welled up.

"It's okay. Just relax now. Everything will come in time. You'll be back to normal before you know it."

The doctor waved for someone, and an African American nurse appeared.

"But I don't know anything. I don't know who I am."

"Are you in any pain?" Dr. Miles asked, in a soothing voice.

"Pain?" she asked, blinking. "Some pain... Yes. But it's not so bad now."

"Good. That's very good. I'm going to give you something to help you sleep," Dr. Miles said, nodding with encouragement. "Don't be frightened. When you awake, I'm sure your memory will have returned, and all will be well."

Anne couldn't have stopped the nurse from giving her the shot, even if she had wanted to—and she didn't want to. She wanted to sleep and never wake up. She was trapped in a nightmare and she couldn't shake it off.

After the nurse drifted away, Dr. Miles clasped his hands before him. "You'll rest well now, and I'll be back to check on you tomorrow."

"What happened to me?" Anne asked abruptly, her head pounding.

Dr. Miles' expression turned serious. "As I said, you were found by a jogger in Central Park, lying in the grass. The jogger called 911."

Anne managed to lift her head a few inches from the pillow. Her eyes were vague and large. "What? 911? What is that? Central Park?"

"... Central Park in New York City."

Anne sank back into the pillow, closing her eyes, and her mind twisted and turned. "I don't know what month or year it is. I don't seem to know. I keep trying to remember, but I can't."

Dr. Miles gently touched her arm. "You've had some traumatic brain injury. Thankfully, it's not severe, so you should get your memory back soon."

Anne glanced down at her arm.

"You also have a dislocated shoulder," Dr. Miles said. "And other injuries, but we'll go over all that later, when you're feeling better."

With her eyes staring up at the ceiling, Anne made fists under the sheet. "What's the month and year?"

"It's October 2008."

As she strained to process his answer, Anne's suffering eyes leveled on his. "You see... I don't know who I am. I should know that, but I don't... I don't know who I am or where I am. I don't know whether I'm a good person or a bad one."

CHAPTER 3

F our days later, Anne sat in a chair by the window, dispirited, gazing out into a gray day, watching snow flurries fly and dance; watching traffic below. She wore a blue hospital gown with a snowflake print, a cotton robe and comfortable fuzzy slippers. Much of her head bandage had been removed and her large shoulder sling had been replaced by a simpler, adjustable sling.

Although she felt better physically, mentally and emotionally she remained bruised, confused and scared. That morning she'd spoken to a psychiatrist, Dr. Helena Weiss, a serious, middle-aged woman with a sturdy build, steady dark eyes and measured speech.

"I want to help you remember," the doctor said. "We will gently look into your past and slowly allow things to be revealed to you in their own time."

Anne stared at the woman, feeling as though she were underwater and trying to come up for air. Nothing looked familiar; nothing seemed right; nothing was being revealed. It was obvious that she was insane. She had completely lost her mind.

Anne was stirred from her troubled thoughts by Dr. Miles, who entered the room and gently cleared his throat. Anne pulled her gaze from the window and looked at him.

"How do you feel today?" Dr. Miles asked.

Anne felt lonely and depressed, but she forced a smile. "I'm much better, thank you."

His smile was again professionally reassuring. He clasped his hands together as he approached. "Well now, I'm very happy to hear it. Your color is good, and your latest tests all show improvement. How was your session with Dr. Weiss this morning?"

"Fine... I just don't remember anything. My mind is a blank."

Dr. Miles nodded, holding his smile. "Not to worry. You did have some swelling on the brain, but there has been improvement. You'll regain your memory soon enough. And the police are actively involved, trying to locate friends or family members."

Anne raised her chin, her eyes hopeful. "And?"

"Nothing so far, but something will turn up. Just give it a little more time."

Anne faced the window with a frown. "Yes, time. But how much longer will it take? I'm lost."

"Things will soon fall into place."

"I'm beginning to wonder."

"Don't give up. Don't push so hard to remember. Relax and let things come as they may."

Anne was lost in her own stare. "The snow is lovely. When I watch it drift by, I get strong feelings and I nearly remember things, but then they flit away so swiftly, before I can grab hold of them, like a dream that fades."

Dr. Miles took a step forward. "One thing we know for sure is that you have a British accent. The police are reaching out to various agencies in the United Kingdom."

Anne seized on that. "Yes, I have noticed the accent. It feels so strange to hear oneself and yet not to know who it is who's speaking. It's quite disconcerting. I must have been coshed on the head."

"Don't worry, something will turn up soon. Meanwhile, I have some good news."

Anne turned to him, waiting.

"I believe I mentioned to you yesterday that there is someone who is paying your hospital bills, including this private room."

"Yes... You told me that she wants to remain anonymous. It is yet another mystery, isn't it, just one more bloody thing I can't solve. That sounds harsh, doesn't it? Sorry."

Dr. Miles clasped his hands together. "Well, this one you *can* solve. She now wants to meet you."

Anne adjusted herself in the chair, her eyes widening. "Does she know me? Does she know who I am?"

"No... I wish I could say she did."

Anne's shoulders drooped. "Then I don't understand. Why? Why would she do this for me if she doesn't know me?"

"Perhaps she wants to tell you herself."

Anne sighed. "What is her name?"

"Mrs. Constance Crowne."

Anne shook her head. "I don't know her. The name means nothing to me."

"She's outside now, waiting. Shall I ask her in?"

Anne looked hesitant, and a little fearful. "Yes... Please."

Dr. Miles left the room while Anne nervously prepared herself. Should she stand? She had a knee brace on her right knee, and she was still wobbly. Whenever she stood too fast, she'd see white spots swimming the room. With some effort, Anne pushed up and steadied herself against the chair.

The door opened, and a tall woman with a dignified manner entered, bringing an air of mystery with her. She was in her middle fifties, dressed richly in a lovely black cashmere coat, burgundy scarf and low heels. Her hair was jet black, styled in a short, layered bob, with highlights of silver and white.

She closed the door, removed her black leather gloves and hesitated. Her gaze was commanding, as if she were used to being in charge, and yet, there was a softness in her eyes. The moment wasn't rushed as she looked Anne over with curiosity and then warm compassion.

"I'm Constance Crowne. Please sit down. You look frail."

Grateful not to stand, Anne lowered herself back down into the chair, sitting stiffly. The room was quiet, and words were elusive, so she forced a smile, hoping the woman recognized her after all.

Mrs. Crowne stepped away from the door, just as it opened. A brawny male nurse's aide entered, carrying a chair. He set it down a few feet from Anne, nodded to both women and left.

Mrs. Crowne slipped out of her coat and scarf and draped them over the back of the chair. Before she sat, she said, "How do you feel?"

Anne held her tentative smile. "I'm feeling better, thank you."

Constance sat, her posture soldier erect. "I detect an English accent."

"Yes... not that I have a clue as to where I come from. But I suppose you know that."

"Yes. Dr. Miles tells me your memory has still not returned," Constance said, noticing Anne's sluggish eyes. "Is it true that you still don't remember your name?"

Anne's smile faded. "I'm afraid so."

Constance nodded. "I'm sorry... I'm sure it's of little comfort to hear others tell you to relax, and that your memory will return in time."

Anne sat up a little straighter. "I have to hope, don't I? Well, a thing like this can make you feel hopeless."

Constance's mind drifted with impressions and theories. There was something about the young woman that touched her, and she recalled what Dr. Miles had said about his patient when she'd first opened her eyes and stared at him. "Her eyes were mad with shock," he'd said.

"I want to thank you for all you've done for me," Anne said. "Dr. Miles said you've paid my hospital bills."

Constance observed that the young woman's face was pale and creased with anxiety. "You're welcome."

Anne looked down at her trembling hands, and in that interval, she tensed. "Forgive me for asking, but do you recognize me?"

Constance smiled affectionately, sadly. "No, I don't. I wish I did, for your sake."

Anne looked away in disappointment. "Then I don't understand..." She lifted a hand and then let it fall into her lap. "Why have you been so generous to me? A nurse told me that this private room is costly."

"The nurse should have kept her mouth shut. It's none of her business," Constance said, bluntly.

Anne's gaze was unsure as it rested on Constance and then wandered the room.

"Do you remember anything?" Constance asked, folding her hands, her voice softening. "Any small thing? Any insignificant thing that might trigger other thoughts and memories?"

Anne looked at Constance shyly. "Just bits and pieces... the fragment of a thought or a fleeting face that darts into the side of my eyes, but I don't know if they're from dreams or from reality... whatever reality is. Right now, I'm not entirely sure what that word means."

The seconds stretched out before Anne finally said, "If you don't know me, Mrs. Crowne, why have you been so generous? I am eternally grateful to you and, of course, I will pay you for all your generosities when I can."

"Don't worry about paying back anything. Right now, your job is to get well, so you can continue on with your life. You are so young and pretty, and you have all your life to live."

Anne was moved by Mrs. Crowne's kindness, and because she felt alone and lost, she fought back tears.

"I suppose you don't remember your age?" Constance asked.

"No... I don't. I feel lost in a fog, and I don't know how to get out."

Constance leaned forward. "Well, you're young and strong and you will heal quickly and completely. Of that I'm positive."

Anne also sat forward, her eyes imploring. "Why have you helped me, Mrs. Crowne? I don't understand. I'm a perfect stranger to you. I don't seem to have anyone, or belong to anyone, and yet you... You have been my angel of mercy. Why?"

To Anne's surprise, Constance's eyes filled with sudden pain, and she lowered them. When she spoke, her voice was emotionally charged.

"A little over a week ago, I had just left the Metropolitan Museum of Art, and I was walking along a path toward the obelisk. It's located behind the Museum. Anyway, I saw a crowd and I could see there was some urgency. Some were on their cell phones and others were crouched down. I started over, concerned, and that's when I saw you lying in the grass, near a tree, not far from the obelisk."

Constance continued. "I heard sirens approach, and more people hurried over. It was those sounds and the gathering crowd that brought it all back. That horrible ordeal. That terrible night that never leaves me."

Mrs. Crowne paused and drew in a breath. "Fifteen years ago, in 1993, my lovely daughter, my only child, Ashley, was found in Central Park, raped and murdered. She'd been jogging and was attacked. She was only eighteen years old."

Anne felt a jolt of agony. "Oh my dear God... I'm so sorry, Mrs. Crowne."

An iron control kept Constance sitting erect, her eyes still. "I will not speak any further about it. I cannot..."

Her fragile words hung in the air, waiting, her face ridged with grief. Constance looked past Anne and out the window at the late autumn sunlight that streamed in, lighting Anne and her lovely face.

Constance fixed her eyes on the young woman. "You are to be discharged tomorrow. Do you have anywhere to go?"

Anne put a shaky hand to her forehead. "No..."

Constance rose, standing erect, a decision made. "Then you will come home with me. My husband, Charles, died a little over a year ago. He was older than I, and he was a wealthy man. In short, I live alone. I'm only telling you this because there is plenty of space and three empty bedrooms. I'm sure you'll be comfortable. You can stay as long as you like, until you recover, or until someone comes forward and identifies you."

Anne was too astonished to speak.

Constance stood firm. "I couldn't help Ashley, but I can certainly help you. We will find your family, and we will find out who you are and where you come from. Meanwhile, let's figure out your sizes and I'll do some basic clothes shopping for you. Once you're better, you can shop for yourself."

Constance smiled, and her eyes twinkled. "We'll make it fun, whoever you are. We'll find out the secrets of you and we'll have a damn good time doing it."

Anne looked fully into Constance's face, her eyes moist, tears breaking free and sliding down her cheeks. "How will I ever thank you?"

CHAPTER 4

On November 1, five days after leaving the hospital, Anne was asleep in her king-sized bed in Constance's East Side townhouse. A knock on the door opened Anne's eyes, and she lifted on elbows, coming out of sleepy consciousness.

"Yes?"

"It's Constance. May I come in?"

Anne sat up. "Yes… Come in."

She tugged the sheet up to her neck, blinking about the spacious room, again overwhelmed by its size and gracious appearance. It was an elegant room, decorated in silver, white and powder blue, with lovely crown molding, thick, silver carpeting, two large, modern mirrors, a crystal chandelier and silver/white draperies adorning three tall windows. Besides the poster bed, there was an extravagant, modern sofa with a matching chair, a broad vanity, and a roomy, private bathroom.

Constance entered the dimly lit room, closing the door softly behind her.

"May I part one of the draperies to let in some light?"

"Yes, of course," Anne said, sleepily.

Constance moved to the first window and pulled one curtain aside, as Anne sat up, squinting against the light.

"Did you sleep well?" Constance asked, turning.

"Yes, much better since my head is free of that bandage. What time is it?"

"It's after nine."

"Oh, I didn't realize it was so late."

"I'm sorry to have awakened you, but I couldn't wait to tell you the good news."

Anne wiped her eyes, suddenly alert and hopeful. "Good news?"

Constance started forward, pausing at the foot of the bed. As always, she was dressed fashionably. Anne admired her black slacks, heels, and silk, silver top, with matching hoop earrings.

"The man I hired to investigate your past called a few minutes ago. He said he had some news, and he's on his way to share it."

Anne's excitement was instant. "Does he know who I am?"

"Not exactly. Anyway, he'll be here at ten-thirty, so I thought you might want to take your shower and eat breakfast before he arrives."

Anne felt the inner tremors start—the same tremors she'd felt in the last few days when her memory had flitted and flashed. She'd tried to grab on and hold any image, name or face, but they had slipped away, like fish diving into deep water, and she was left frustrated and scared. What if she never remembered?

"You look anxious," Constance said. "Don't be. Let's keep treating your mystery as a fun adventure. Let's keep it light and let's keep it exciting."

Anne smiled, grateful. "Thank you, Constance. I don't know what I would do without you."

"You've given me a new purpose, and a new life," Constance said warmly. "And since you moved in, I'm even humming again. I haven't hummed my tuneless song since before Charles died. I'm delighted you're here. Now, I'm going to leave and let you start your day. I'll have Agnes make you some breakfast. What will you have? Eggs? Oatmeal?"

"Just some oatmeal and toast."

"And tea, I'm sure?"

"Yes, tea would be lovely. English Breakfast, since you have it."

Constance wagged a finger at Anne. "I think we know one thing about you. Your English accent and your love for tea must surely mean you're originally from the United Kingdom."

Constance's words had a striking impact. Anne shut her eyes. She made a little sound of recognition when swimming letters splashed across the screen of her mind. They swelled, then faded, then appeared again, then vanished.

Anne drew in a sharp breath and, with a hand, she touched her breast near her jumping heart.

"What is it?" Constance asked. "Are you all right?"

Anne's eyes opened and widened. "I just heard a name jump into my head. Someone spoke it to me. It was a man's voice, and it was loud before it faded. The name seems so right, and so familiar to me."

"What was the name?"

Anne tip-toed her mind back to the man's voice and to the name he'd called out. "I heard a voice call Anne."

Constance waited, and the room was silent and still.

Anne touched her neck, her face flushed. "I heard it. I heard the name… It was Anne. Yes, I heard the name Anne so clearly and I wanted to answer. I recognized it as mine and I wanted to answer."

Constance went to the side of the bed and took Anne's hand. She held it, looking into Anne's hopeful eyes.

"Here's what I'm going to do. I'm going to start calling you Anne. Let's see if, by repetition, it begins to sink in deeper until it resonates; until you're completely sure. Perhaps a last name will also come soon. How does that sound… Anne?"

Anne held Constance's stare, worried. She nodded. "Yes, why not Anne?"

Constance released Anne's hand and stepped back. "I think we should both congratulate ourselves. We're making progress. Who knows what will come next? See what a great adventure this is becoming?"

A lonely fear returned to Anne, but she hid it from Constance. Anne thought, *What if I just imagined the voice and the name? What if I am desperately trying to reconstruct a false self from my imagination? That would be a kind of insanity, wouldn't it?*

Constance clapped her hands together. "All right, take your shower, Anne, and I'll meet you downstairs."

When Constance opened the door to leave, Anne called after her. "Constance…"

Constance glanced back.

"I don't quite know how to say it, but I don't feel… well, I don't feel properly anchored in my skin, or in this world. Everything seems so unfamiliar and strange. That television, the cell phone you gave me, all the cars and the fashion. I feel out of place… as though I shouldn't be here."

Constance took a step back into the room, lowering her voice in sympathy. "Dr. Miles wants to make a house call this afternoon, Anne. And Dr. Weiss is coming as well. She said your memory might return all at once, or in bits and pieces. Tell them everything you feel, and they'll help you. Trust, Anne. Trust that everything will work out. We will get to the bottom of this sooner or later."

Anne sat back, a little smile forming. "It feels right... I mean, my name. Anne feels right... and with an E. Yes, Anne with an E I think is spot-on."

"It suits you," Constance said. "I like it very much. All right, I'll see you downstairs."

Constance flashed a final, mischievous little grin. "As Sherlock Holmes would say, 'The game's still afoot.'"

CHAPTER 5

They sat in the soft blue furniture of an expansive living room, looking out onto the magnificent skyline of Manhattan from the twenty-second floor. In the white marble fireplace, a gleaming fire added comfort, warmth and elegance.

Anne was seated on the sofa next to Constance, dressed in designer jeans, a light green top, and a white cashmere cardigan. She was trying to stop her hands from twisting in her lap as she studied Leon Fogle. He was a thin, wiry young man in his late twenties, slumped in a chair opposite them, his Apple iPad at the ready, his black-rimmed glasses pushed up on his nose, his face projecting fervent concentration. He resembled Daniel Radcliffe, the actor who played Harry Potter, and before he arrived, Constance admitted that that was one reason she'd hired him. Leon had also come highly recommended by a friend's son, a technology executive.

Anne was surprised by Leon. She thought him much too young for what he had been asked to do, which was to find out who she was and where she'd come from.

Constance sat up, inclining toward him, her face pointed at him with sharp interest.

"On the phone, Leon, you said you might have something."

Leon's mouth twitched. He blinked frequently, his little squirrel eyes shifting from Constance to Anne and from Anne to Constance. The silence grew as a siren passed below, and a log shifted in the fireplace, hissing and popping.

Anne studied Leon's clothing. His sneakers were a faded red, his jeans a faded blue, and his sweater so tight it looked as if it had shrunk. And he had a bad case of bedhead, with little tufts of brown hair shooting up from a cowlick.

"Yes, well, Mrs. Crowne, I used the photo you had taken of..." he searched for a name.

"Anne," Constance said, turning to Anne and indicating with a gesture. "This is Anne."

Leon nodded rapidly. "Anne. Yeah, cool. I didn't have that. Yeah, well, as I told you when you hired me, since you didn't have a full name, or any name, or any relative or employer or a social security number, and all that other necessary stuff, I went with a reverse image search."

"And what is that?" Constance asked.

Leon adjusted his glasses, lowering his tenor voice to sound more authoritative.

"The technology is still relatively new, and it's being improved continuously, but I've found it very useful. Anyway, a reverse image search is a type of search engine technology. That is, you use an image file as an input query. You upload the image to the software and it constantly crawls the web and adds images to its index.

The database has more than three billion images that it scrapes from *Facebook*, *YouTube*, *Venmo* and millions of other websites. The software I use debunks any faked images so the matches I get are actual, or close to actual."

"And what did you find?" Constance asked, wanting to cut to the chase.

"I received several images that were close to Anne's image, but none that were a match, or not even in the ninetieth percentile. So I rejected them all."

Anne looked at him with tender sadness. "Are these results unusual? Has this ever happened to you before?"

Leon adjusted his glasses again, pushing them higher on his nose. He cleared his throat. "No. It's never happened, and that's like... wow, you know."

Anne's face fell, but Constance noticed Leon's eyes were bright with anticipation.

"Is there more, Leon?" Constance asked.

"Well, it's just that, I think it's real cool. I mean, like I said, this is the first time this has ever happened to me."

Anne sat back with a small breath of acceptance, and turned her eyes to the fire, getting lost in the flames.

Constance was annoyed by his choice of words. "Leon, it is *not* cool that you haven't found Anne's identity. You're obviously doing something wrong or you're just not up to the job I gave you. Anne is here, right here in the flesh, so she *has* to be in one of your databases. At her age, she has to be on social media or, I don't know, on something. So all your computer databases must be wrong or you're doing something wrong."

Leon leaned forward, stuttering. "No, no... Well, of course, that's not cool, Mrs. Crowne, I only meant that it's a real mystery, you know? That's what's cool about it. And, no, the software I use is the best, and it's always worked for me. The algorithms don't miss. If Anne is anywhere on social media, it would have tossed out a match right away. But it didn't. No match."

Constance's eyes wouldn't let him go. She was fascinated and impressed that he was undaunted by his failure. "So what do you plan to do now, Leon?"

"I called my uncle. He's with the CIA. They have these powerful databases that reach back years, even before computers—like all the way to the 1940s and further. I've already called him. He said he'd run Anne's photo. So I sent it to him."

Constance readjusted herself as she lowered her eyes in thought. She grew guarded and remote.

For the first time since she'd met Constance, Anne saw that she looked worried and concerned, and Constance's expression and Leon's failure felt like weights pressing down on her.

When Constance raised her eyes to Leon, he was alert, sitting at attention.

"All right, Leon, speculate for me. How could this be? If you've done all your computer searching and didn't find a match, then why and how could that be?"

He shrugged. "I don't know. At the very least, Anne should have some kind of photo ID, from a college or a passport, or a visa, or a driver's license, or a security card issued by an employer. Yeah, well, it's a mystery. And by now, I thought a relative or friend or, I don't know, a husband or a boyfriend would have shown up."

Constance glanced at Anne and grew uneasy. She recalled something Dr. Miles had said to her the day after Anne had been admitted, when she lay close to death.

"Something doesn't seem quite right," he'd said. "A couple of the nurses told me that the injured woman's clothes are very retro. They think she must have been acting in a play. The police took a photo of the woman and they're going to show it around to some of the Broadway directors and actors."

Constance hadn't mentioned it to Anne, but maybe she should have. Maybe it would have helped jog her memory. The police had come up empty. None of the actors or directors recognized Anne.

Anne was cold with anxiety while Leon stared into his iPad. She finally asked, "When is your uncle supposed to contact you?"

"I don't know," Leon answered. "He said he'd get to it when he could."

AFTER CONSTANCE SAW LEON OUT, she returned to the living room to find Anne slumped over, her face in her hands, quietly weeping.

"Now, now, Anne," Constance said, stepping over to place a comforting hand on her shoulder. "Don't cry, my dear. It's going to work out."

Anne removed her hands from her face. Her eyes were damp, her expression painfully sad. Constance went to the coffee table, drew several tissues from a blue, ornate tissue dispenser and took them to Anne.

While Anne dabbed at her eyes, Constance eased down beside her, composing the question she wanted to ask. She'd have to pose it gently, so as not to startle the fragile young woman.

"Anne…"

Anne stared ahead, her eyes unfocused.

"Does the name Anne still sound familiar to you?"

"Yes…"

"Good. Very good.

Constance softened her voice. "Anne, I want to tell you something I learned from Dr. Miles the day after you were admitted to the Intensive Care Unit."

Anne sat up, a tissue balled in her hand.

"Dr. Miles told me that when the police spoke to him, well, I should say the detectives, they told the doctor that the dress you were wearing had a label. The label read Bourne & Hollingsworth, Oxford Street."

Constance studied Anne's face for some sign of recognition. She saw none, so she continued. "The detectives learned that the department store Bourne & Hollingsworth closed in 1983. The building is currently occupied by the Bourne & Hollingsworth Bar."

Anne looked to Constance, waiting for further explanation.

"I saw the dress, Anne. Although it was soiled and torn in places, it was a lovely dress. One of the detectives described it as 'clearly retro.' By that, he meant its style was from the 1940s, a classic bottle green crepe, with a slim waist and boxy shoulders. I know that because I used the internet to find similar dresses on *Google*."

"*Google*?" Anne asked.

Constance was startled. "You must know what *Google* is, Anne. At your age, surely you've used *Google* to search for things."

"No, I don't know what it is."

Constance waved a hand of dismissal and pushed ahead. "Okay, it doesn't matter. Anyway, your shoes were black leather pumps, and the inside label said Bishops Styles of West London. After doing some research online, the detectives learned that the shoe store was bombed into ruins in 1942."

Anne rose and went to the fireplace, staring into it. "I don't know, Constance. I don't know what you're saying or what you want from me. I don't know those places. I've never heard of them. I must be going insane."

Constance pushed up and went to her. "Anne... I brought it up because I hoped it might help you remember. Everything can be explained. I'm sure there's a perfectly good reason for all of it."

Anne faced her. "What reason? How can anything be explained when I don't even seem to exist?"

"Maybe you were an actress, Anne," Constance said. "That would account for the clothes. Do you have any memory of that?"

Anne shook her head. "No, I don't remember. I just don't know. When I was in the hospital, and the police were asking me all those questions and I had no answers, I saw the look in their eyes. They thought I was hiding something, or protecting someone, or they thought I was insane. So, yes, maybe I'm insane. Maybe it's that simple."

"You're not, Anne. You're not insane."

Anne moved back to the couch and sat, staring out the windows. "Dr. Weiss said she could try hypnotizing me. If I'm a good candidate, she might be able to take me back to the time before I was found in the park, and I might reveal who I am."

Constance nodded. "Yes, she shared that with me yesterday on the phone. Then you've decided to try it... today? When she comes?"

"Yes. I'm desperate. I'll do whatever I need to do. I can't live like this. I feel lost and helpless and useless. Just before I fall asleep, and just before I awaken, I see faces and hear sounds, terrible sounds, and it all seems so close and yet so very far away."

Anne held her head in her hands. "I have to remember. I have to, or I'm going to shatter into pieces."

CHAPTER 6

"I NEVER MAKE HOUSE CALLS," Dr. Miles said, smiling, as he shrugged out of his overcoat and handed it to the middle-aged, West Indian maid, Clarisse. A handsome man, he was dressed in gray slacks, a blue shirt and royal blue sport coat. His hair was combed to one side and parted low, a new stylish look. With his dimples and intoxicating hazel eyes, he could have easily played the part of any doctor in any soap opera, and the women viewers would have adored him.

Constance took his arm and led him slowly through the marble foyer, down a short hallway, toward the living room.

"I suspect, Jon, that your primary interest for being here is not medical, but romantic."

"Though we're good friends, I'll not answer that, Constance. I'll simply ask, how is the patient?"

Constance stopped, frowning, lowering her voice. "Physically she's much better, even remarkably better... I'm calling her Anne, and that is with an E, or so she told me. She said that name sounds familiar to her."

"Just Anne? Nothing more?"

"No, nothing more."

"Is she waiting?"

"She's in her room, resting. I said I'd let her know when you and Dr. Weiss arrive. Let's go into the living room and have a glass of wine. There's a dry white Burgundy chilling in the wine bucket."

Minutes later, Jon Miles stood by the tall windows, swirling his glass of wine, watching snow flurries flit by as Constance paced behind the sofa, sipping at her wine, filling him in on what had occurred that morning.

Dr. Miles turned to Constance with a perplexed expression. "Well, Anne couldn't have just dropped in from out of thin air," he said. "How could there be no image match? That seems nearly impossible in this day and age. Did she respond when you told her about the dress and shoes?"

Constance shrugged a shoulder. "No... Nothing. And she's never heard of *Google*, so there has to be some amnesia going on. Isn't that clear enough?"

"We did all the imaging tests—including an MRI and a CT scan—to check for brain damage or abnormalities," Jon said. "There was nothing. Her blood tests came out fine, and an electroencephalogram didn't find any presence of seizure activity."

Constance looked around searching for things to say; for things that might explain the oddities of Anne's predicament. "Anne said something so poignant to me earlier. She said, 'I feel like a badly functioning marionette.'"

Dr. Miles sighed. "Perhaps Helena will have some luck with hypnosis. Is Anne limping?"

"Not much. She said the pain has diminished, and she's very anxious to let her hair grow. She said she always wore it long, down on her shoulders."

Dr. Miles lifted an eyebrow. "That's an interesting detail to recall."

Constance grinned, knowingly. "Jon, please... Women always remember hairstyles and makeup."

"I'm anxious to see her."

"I'm going to be blunt, Jon. Do you plan to ask her out?"

"Of course," and before Constance could respond, he raised a hand in a placating manner. "I'm not going to continue as her doctor, so there won't be any doctor/patient issue. I'm recommending Dr. Lambert."

"I don't know him."

"Her. Dr. Sharon Lambert. She's good. You'll like her."

"How old is she?"

"In her forties. More importantly, I think Anne will like her. I told Dr. Lambert I'd arrange an appointment whenever you and Anne are ready."

There was speculation in the tilt of Constance's head. "I don't know about this."

"Look, Constance, I'm divorced with no children and I haven't been out on a date in, oh, let's see now, three months. And frankly, I like Anne. I'd like to get to know her better, and maybe I can help her remember details of her life."

Constance brushed his comments aside. "Just be sure to tell this Dr. Lambert that I don't want Anne going through a lot of therapy or taking so many drugs that she gets lost and we never find her again."

"I understand. I'll tell her. Better yet, you can tell her when you meet."

Just then Clarisse appeared, escorting Dr. Helena Weiss into the living room.

"There you are," Constance said, starting toward the doctor. "I'm so glad you could come. Would you like a glass of white Burgundy?"

Dr. Weiss entered the room, brisk and businesslike, toting a black leather shoulder bag, dressed in a casual gray suit, white blouse and black pumps. She was slightly flushed, had a pensive mouth, and seemed mildly irritated.

"No, thank you, Constance. I've been trapped in traffic inside an awful smelling taxi, with a driver who spoke little English, not that that stopped his incessant chatter and, if that wasn't enough, the pitiful man had a terminal case of bad breath."

"Well, then, you must have a glass of wine."

Dr. Weiss waved her off. "No, I have to be clear-headed while I work."

Dr. Weiss gave her regards to Dr. Miles, then glanced about. "Now, where is the patient?"

"She's resting in her room. I'll go get her," Constance said, striding across the living room toward the back rooms. She stopped and turned. "Oh, I wanted to tell you. She remembers her first name. It's Anne."

Dr. Weiss arched an eyebrow. "Well, that's a start. Yes. That's a very good start. I can use that in hypnosis."

Ten minutes later, Constance returned with Anne, who entered the room and then paused when she noticed Dr. Miles smiling at her and Dr. Weiss studying her.

To Dr. Weiss, Anne appeared tired, her face registering a weary sense of dread. Dr. Weiss took a few steps toward her. "I'm so happy to see you up and around and looking better. Constance tells me you've remembered your first name. So, I should say, it's good to see you again, Anne."

Anne nodded. "Thank you, Dr. Weiss."

Dr. Weiss turned to Constance. "Now, where can Anne and I go to have our session?"

Constance tried to contain her excitement as she gestured toward the hallway. "Follow me to the den. It was Charles' favorite room, and it's comfortable and private."

As the ladies started toward the den, Dr. Miles spoke up, and the women paused.

"Anne..."

Anne turned, constrained by apprehension.

"I'd like to talk to you after your session with Dr. Weiss," Jon said.

Constance's mouth twitched. Dr. Weiss was impatient.

"Yes... Of course, Dr. Miles."

"Assuming that she's up to it," Constance cautioned.

Jon's mouth tightened. "Of course. That goes without saying."

"Well, let's get to it," Dr. Weiss said, now leading the way, even though she wasn't sure where the room was.

With a grand gesture, Constance opened the double wooden doors which led to the spacious den. Decorated in a modern style, it had an elegant, glass-topped coffee table with a lavish bouquet of fresh flowers in the center. Dark gray area rugs with abstract designs covered much of the polished wood floors. Resting on them were a black leather sofa and matching chairs. Soft gray drapes were drawn against the natural light, and subdued track lighting washed the room. A wide, wall-mounted TV covered one wall, and sleek white bookshelves ran the length of another side of the room. Its hardback and leather-bound books were encased in glass. The white marble fireplace was banked low. Opposite the bookshelves, the door to a private bathroom was open, revealing emerald tiles and a mirrored wall.

Constance stood by, as Dr. Weiss pointed to the sofa.

"Please make yourself comfortable, Anne, while I take out the recorder and my supplies."

"A recorder?" Anne asked.

"Yes. I'll use it for my analysis. I'll be happy to make a copy for you, if you'd like."

Anne's eyes focused on the digital recorder. "It's small, isn't it?"

"Yes, but it has exceptionally good fidelity. Please sit down, Anne," Dr. Weiss said, and then she moved her attention to Constance. "You may go now, Constance. Thank you."

Folding her hands, Constance reluctantly left the room, shutting the door behind her. She lingered in the hallway, feeling curiosity and concern arise in equal measures. She'd grown very attached to Anne. She wanted to protect her, spoil her, and love her as she could no longer love her dead daughter, Ashley, whose violent death remained an open wound in her soul.

Constance dared a smile. To feel needed, to feel real love coursing again through her veins, was like a soothing drug. These were feelings she'd hungered for and been without for too long, feelings she might never have again.

I will keep Anne in my life, no matter where she comes from or who she turns out to be, Constance thought. Anne needed all the help, protection and love Constance could give her.

She leaned back against the door, desperate to know what was going on inside that room. Would Anne emerge from the session, beaming with tentative joy as the first hints of her identity became known? If that happened, then what would come next? Constance felt a twist of anguish. Anne might leave.

Constance's heart beat all the faster. Of course she would leave, and Constance would be happy for her, wouldn't she?

Constance stood upright, blinking. If it was inevitable for Anne to leave, then as long as she was living with Constance, she wanted her all to herself. Only she could provide the safety and emotional protection she required. The last thing Constance needed was for Jon Miles, with his silly infatuation, to insinuate himself into their lives, especially now, when Anne was so very vulnerable. That was out of the question.

When Constance returned to the living room, Jon noted her darkened mood. Hers was the expression of someone who had just discovered a torment that she'd had no idea was inside her.

"Is everything all right, Constance?"

She didn't look up. "I think you should go, Jon."

Jon cocked an ear. "Excuse me, did you say, go?"

"Yes. This is not the time for romance. You'll just confuse her."

"Can I at least wait to see what Dr. Weiss discovers?"

Constance lifted her frosty eyes on him. "I think you should go."

Jon gave her a long moment of consideration. "All right, Constance, if you think it's best."

As he was leaving the room, he said. "Will you let me know if Anne remembers anything?"

Constance didn't look at him. "That depends."

Dr. Miles ran a hand along his jaw. "Constance, I am going to ask Anne out. I think it will be good for her. You can't lock her away."

Constance didn't look at him.

When he was gone, she lowered herself down on the sofa and turned her head toward the den, thrusting her mind back to the first time she'd seen Anne, looking so scared and helpless. Constance struggled to tamp down her emotions, even as an image of Ashley appeared, then slowly melted away.

.

CHAPTER 7

"GENTLY CLOSE YOUR EYES, Anne, and relax," Dr. Weiss said.

Anne lay on the sofa, her hands resting at her sides, a white cotton blanket covering her. Dr. Weiss sat in a chair a few feet away, a legal pad and pen at the ready and her recorder lying on the broad arm of the chair.

"Now, Anne, I want you to focus on your breathing. Just watch the breath come in and out, in and out. Feel the comfort and support of the breath and, as you do so, say to yourself, relax."

Anne obeyed.

Dr. Weiss continued. "Now, I want you to inhale deep, and breathe out long. Repeat that four times and, as you exhale, I want you to say to yourself: Body, relax."

Anne readjusted herself and inhaled her first breath.

"Feel your silky breath come and go, and allow every muscle to soften as you breathe out."

Anne listened and tried to follow Dr. Weiss' instructions, but stress pooled in her stomach, and her mind was alive with racing thoughts and fleeting images.

"Just relax, Anne. Everything is fine. Breathe easy and relax."

Minutes later, Dr. Weiss leaned in, lowering her voice. "Now, Anne, I want you to focus only on the sound of my voice. Nothing else. No sounds other than my voice. Okay?"

"Yes… okay."

Dr. Weiss guided Anne into deeper states of relaxation, until the doctor observed that Anne's face muscles were relaxed, and her breathing was even and calm.

"Anne, I want you to feel as though you're floating. In your imagination, float up and up into a pristine, warm, deep blue sky and merge with the soft, white, puffy clouds. Do that now."

Dr. Weiss waited, alert. "Are you floating, Anne?"

"Yes…"

"Good. Just drift with those clouds for a while as you relax and go even deeper."

Anne did go deeper, allowing herself to float and drift in and out of clouds. When she spoke, her voice was a whisper. "The white clouds above are floating pillows and I'm moving in and out of them, riding a gentle breeze."

"That's very good, Anne… Now, listen very carefully. I want you to let yourself go and travel anywhere that pleases you. Let go and fly off to any place you wish. Anywhere at all. Do that now."

It was a command that appealed to Anne. It was permission to escape, and she longed to escape from her lost, confused and bizarre world of shadows.

In a quiet, timeless state, Anne felt as though she were under water, and yet airy and light like a moving cloud.

"Where are you, Anne?"

Anne didn't seem to have a body and, instead of this scaring her, she found it amusing. She was a feather, a floating yellow balloon, a soaring bird.

"Anne? Do you hear my voice?"

Anne didn't want to talk. She was peaceful, warm and light.

Dr. Weiss continued. "Anne, tell me, where are you? What are you feeling? What are you seeing?"

At first, everything was a blur, like an abstract painting, with merging colors, odd shapes and shifting designs. But then, slowly, a picture began to take shape. Anne saw flickering lights circling her, filling the sky and the earth, washing across the sea. The colored lights were so beautiful and cheerful.

"What are you seeing, Anne? Tell me. Where are you right now?"

Anne cleared her throat, her voice barely audible. "I see... lights... Yes, moving, swirling lights."

"Good. What is the source of the lights? Can you see the source of the lights?"

"I don't know... Wait. I... Yes. Wait..."

"Take your time, Anne. What is the source of the lights?"

Anne's voice grew soft with wonder. "Oh look... I'm at a dance. I'm looking up and I see a mirror ball suspended from the ceiling."

"A mirror ball? What is that?"

"You know, a mirror ball. There's a large revolving ball on the ceiling, covered with small pieces of mirror that reflect the light, and the patterns keep changing." Anne smiled happily. "Oh, yes. It's lit up, and tiny circles of light are floating all around. Oh, it's so magical and romantic. There's a crowd of people on the dance floor and... Yes, and I hear music now. I know that music... It's a big band playing swing music."

"Swing music?"

"Yes, swing music. I love this song."

"What is the song, Anne? What is the name of the song?"

Anne didn't speak. Her eyes fluttered.

"What's the song, Anne?"

"I remember this song... Yes. I..." Anne's voice faded, leaving a pleasant smile.

"Where is this dance? Look around and see if you can see a name."

"I don't know. Such fun... and..." Her voice trailed off once more.

"What's the name of the song, Anne?"

"The song? Oh, it's *That Old Black Magic...* That's it... Glenn Miller... I heard it on the radio. I was... we danced..."

"Are you with anyone, Anne? Do you see yourself with anyone?"

Anne's eyelids twitched. She lifted a weak hand. "With... anyone?"

"Yes, at the dance. Are you standing next to anyone?"

Anne was silent, her eyes continuing to flutter, her mouth to twitch.

Dr. Weiss reached for a tissue and blotted her lower lip, steadying herself with an effort. She wasn't entirely sure what was going on. Was Anne dreaming, hallucinating, remembering a childhood memory? Dr. Weiss needed confirmation of time and place.

"Anne... How are the people dressed? Is it a formal dance?"

"Uniforms... Mostly all in uniforms."

"What kind of uniforms?"

"You must know... Why are you asking me? There is a war going on, you know."

Dr. Weiss sat back. "A war? What kind of war... I mean, what war is it?"

Anne moved her head slightly. "It's another world war, of course, like the Great War."

Dr. Weiss stiffened. "What?"

Anne's voice saddened. "Yes... and it's so dreadful."

"A world war, did you say?"

"Everyone is braving it, bucking up, showing the old British stiff upper lip."

Dr. Weiss' voice was tight in her throat. "Anne, what year is it? Please tell me the year."

"What a thing to ask... Everyone knows that," Anne said, with some irritation.

"Well, I don't know it. Please tell me. What is the year?"

Anne's voice fell into a hollow sadness. "Oh, God. Captain Raffety has just told us the terrible news..."

"What news, Anne? Tell me what the news is, now."

"The German Luftwaffe came again, and they devastated Birkenhead and Liverpool. The docks and shipyards have been ravaged, along with several hospitals. Oh, it's so awful. Many hundreds of civilians were killed, and thousands are homeless."

Tears leaked from Anne's eyes and raced down her cheeks. "When will this terrible war end?"

Dr. Weiss' hands began to tremble, her voice shaky. "Anne... Tell me where you are, and what year it is. Tell me, now."

Anne struggled to get the words out. "I'm in England, at a dance near Oxford. It's October 1942."

Dr. Weiss looked stricken.

CHAPTER 8

"I DON'T KNOW WHAT to make of it," Dr. Weiss said, pacing the living room, a glass of wine in her hand.

Constance sat on the sofa, her eyes fixed on the doctor, who was noticeably upset.

"You must have some idea, Doctor."

Dr. Weiss stopped. "Oh, I have some idea, alright, but I don't like it and I don't believe in it. It's all the rage. Regression therapy, past lives and reincarnation."

"But did you find out Anne's full name?"

Dr. Weiss looked down and away, as if ashamed. "Well... No. I was going to, but..."

Constance cut her off. "... I'd think that would be the first thing you'd ask."

"Well, I didn't," Dr. Weiss snapped.

The silence stretched out until the quiet began to hurt.

Dr. Weiss swallowed the rest of her wine and set the empty glass down on the coffee table. "I meant to ask her. It's just that I was, well, I was startled by the bizarre direction of the session. I'd expected her to talk about her childhood or a vivid memory from her past. I just didn't know what to make of it. And Anne went under so easily. The next thing I knew, she was talking about World War Two... and in detail. It unnerved me. I'm a traditional psychotherapist, and entirely skeptical of therapists who claim that, under hypnosis, their clients recall past lives and past-life traumas. To me, that falls under the category of pseudo-science, fantasy, wishful thinking or, I don't know, wild imagination."

Constance rose and strolled toward the bank of windows that looked out onto the gray Manhattan skyline, the towers obscured by low clouds. Dr. Weiss stood in a subdued awkwardness, eyeing the bottle of wine still chilling in the bucket.

Constance clasped her hands behind her back and made a small frown of concentration. "Dr. Weiss, when I took Anne to her room after the session, she was pale, she was crying, and she wouldn't talk to me. She dropped onto the bed and instantly fell to sleep."

Constance turned. "Something happened to Anne and I think it's obvious that, whatever it was, it was not average or ordinary. Why was she wearing those 1940s clothes? Why hasn't anyone come forward to identify her? Why doesn't she have any identification or even one photograph that can be traced by the latest technology?"

Constance's gaze wandered. "When you brought Anne out of hypnosis, did she remember anything she'd told you? Anything at all?"

"I told you. She wouldn't speak to me. I asked her several times if she was all right and if she remembered, but she just sat on that sofa, staring blankly ahead."

"You must have another session with her," Constance said, directly. "And you must ask her her name and who her family is and where she was born. All of those things."

Dr. Weiss looked at Constance disapprovingly. "I do not appreciate being ordered about and told what I must do, Mrs. Crowne. Frankly, I am not comfortable working with this young woman, and going forward, I advise you to find another therapist."

Constance was incredulous. "You must be joking."

"I am not joking. Not in the least."

Dr. Weiss turned and picked up her bag. "I wish you a good afternoon."

Constance watched Dr. Weiss march out of the living room and down the hallway toward the front door. After she was gone, Constance remained standing, considering everything that had occurred, every stray detail. The more she thought about it, the more she was convinced that Dr. Weiss' abrupt decision to suspend Anne's treatment was a blessing. The woman was obviously deficient and simply not up to the job.

Constance would find a doctor who was up to the challenge, and she'd get to the bottom of Anne's story, if it was the last thing she ever did.

But as soon as that thought had arisen and fallen, and just as she was about to pick up the phone to call a doctor friend, another thought, sharper and illuminating, struck. She did not reach for her cell phone. Instead, she stood very still, her calculating eyes not moving.

"I don't need to know what happened," Constance said aloud. Then she thought, *It doesn't matter. Whatever happened to Anne under regression, it had been traumatic.*

Constance eased down on the sofa, resisting the urge to pour another glass of wine. She needed a clear head to think. The more Anne remembered who she was and where she'd come from, the sooner she'd leave. Of course she would. She'd return to her family and friends, to her old life. But if she didn't recall, perhaps, yes, just perhaps, she never would remember, and the old memories would eventually disappear like a rock dropped into deep water. Constance found the thought guiltily appealing. Anne not remembering her past could turn out to be a blessing. Anne could build a new and wonderfully fulfilling life, with Constance at the center of it.

Constance rose to her feet and wandered the room. Her thoughts ignited with plans and possibilities. Instead of hypnosis and doctors and the strain of remembering, it would be better for Anne, and for Constance, if Anne didn't recall—and never recalled—anything from her past.

If Constance could help Anne build a new life from the ground up, become imbedded and involved in life in the present, surely Anne would soon lose her desire to remember. Constance would ensure that Anne was completely and utterly happy in her new life, not wanting for anything.

Constance absently ran a hand through her hair, pleased with her new strain of thought, galvanized by the potential. There would be no more solitary nights or days seeking a reason to exist, batting away bitterness and rage at God, or whoever controls mortals and the universe or, more accurately, doesn't control them; lets them run wild is more like it. Why would any kind of compassionate God let a beautiful girl like Ashley die in such a brutal way?

Anne had already given Constance a reason to breathe, and smile, and hum a no-tune song. Constance had not prayed in a very long time, but whenever she thought of Anne, she involuntarily fell into a prayer of thanksgiving, grateful that Anne had miraculously appeared in her life.

Her burst of happiness vanished when she acknowledged that she was in emotional danger. She knew she'd become inextricably attached to Anne; attached and in love, like a mother finding a brand-new daughter who needed guidance, support, and a mother's love. She heaved in a breath and blew it out, as if to blow out the burning candle of her emotions. She did it twice more, until her mind had cooled.

Then she calmly and stoically reversed her thinking about Dr. Jon Miles. He could be the perfect distraction for Anne—a romantic encounter that would help anchor her in the present.

When Constance reached for her cell phone to call Jon, expectation hung in the air. The expectation that she and Anne could enjoy a long, loving and rewarding life together surged from deep within her soul.

"Hello, Jon… It's Constance."

"Constance. What's happened? Is Anne all right?"

"Yes, quite all right. She's resting."

"How was the session? Did she reveal anything about her past?"

"Not much. I'll tell you all about it later. Look, forgive me today for my rudeness. I've been under stress and not myself. I apologize for my behavior."

"I understand. You were abrupt, and I got the message. I'll stay away from Anne until she's stronger."

"On the contrary, Jon. I think what Anne needs is an adventure. It would do her a world of good."

There was silence on the other end.

"Jon, are you there?"

"I am. What has caused this sudden change of mind, Constance?"

"I told you. I've been thinking about it. Anne needs to get out of her frightened, protective shell and have some fun. I know it's just what she needs, and you're the right person to show her a good time. I know you're fond of her."

"Yes, Constance, I am. All right. When do you suggest I ask Anne out on a formal date?"

"The sooner the better. Why don't you call her tonight, say around eight o'clock? Ask her out to dinner for tomorrow night."

"Are you going to be our chaperon, Constance?" Jon asked, lightly.

"Don't be sarcastic, Jon. It doesn't suit you. You have a good bedside manner because you are dedicated and true. Stay with that. All your women patients fall for you and, who knows, in time, Anne might fall for you too."

"And a matchmaker, too?" Jon said, surprise in his voice.

"I can be whatever I need to be, Jon, and right now I want Anne to be healthy and happy. So, we'll be expecting your call. Good bye now."

Constance hung up, her smile inwardly triumphant. She started for Anne's bedroom, holding the smile, feeling more invigorated and optimistic than she had in years. Anne was going to have a good life—the life of a princess—filled with love and opportunity. Constance would shower her with jewels, with clothes and exotic journeys. Perhaps Anne would find Jon attractive, and they would get involved in a relationship. That would be all right, too, as long as they didn't take the relationship too far. At least not for a few years.

When Constance opened Anne's bedroom door to check on her, she was giddy with plans and satisfaction. Constance peered in. Anne wasn't in her bed.

Concerned, Constance entered, casting her eyes about the dimly lit room. When she saw Anne, she screamed. "Anne!"

Anne was standing outside the window on the broad window ledge, staring down from the twenty-second floor, her silk, diaphanous gown billowing in the wind.

With her face contorted in horror, Constance tore off across the room toward the window.

CHAPTER 9

Anne was in bed, the quilt drawn up to her chin, her cheeks flushed red from standing outside on the window ledge in the cold, blustery wind.

"I wasn't going to jump," Anne said. "I only wanted to feel the wind and see the wide expanse of the city. I thought it might help me to remember; to put all the pieces together."

Constance knelt at her bedside, her pulse still racing. When she'd seen Anne standing outside on the window ledge, she'd made a mad dash across the room, seized Anne's left wrist and tugged her back into the room. Both women went tumbling, sprawling onto the carpet, Anne breathless, Constance trying to recover her wits.

"Don't do that again, Anne," Constance scolded. "You nearly gave me a heart attack. A gust of wind could have sent you plummeting to your death."

Anne looked at Constance tenderly. "I'm sorry. I didn't mean to give you a fright." She turned her head away and seemed to go to a small, sad place.

"Was the session that disturbing, Anne?"

Anne didn't look at her. "I feel shattered and groping—even more now. That session with Dr. Weiss scared me and confused me. The faces, the sounds, and the music all seemed to be trapped in a mirror and, as I watched, I wanted to reach out; I wanted to step inside that mirror and join in. I felt a part of that world, but I couldn't break through."

Anne heaved out a deep sigh. "Oh, I know I'm not making any sense," she said, cushioning her head into the pillow, staring up at the ceiling. "What is the matter with me? Why can't I remember my past and who I am?"

"Well, do you know what? You don't have to remember, Anne. You don't have to remember any of it. The more I've been thinking about it, the more I think you're fortunate."

Anne rolled her head to meet Constance's eyes. "Fortunate?"

"Do you know how many people in this world would love to forget their past? I, for one. I wish I never had another thought about my daughter or that awful time. I'd love to forget that Charles suffered for months before he died. So, yes, it's a blessing and a gift that you've forgotten. You should let the past go completely and embrace the present, fully."

Anne knitted her brows. "But I truly want to remember, Constance, and I must remember. I must know who I am and where I came from."

Constance had an answer ready, having imagined this conversation only an hour ago. "Then I say, the best way to remember is to stop trying. Stop straining. Stop trying to remember anything. It's when we relax and let go that buried thoughts, ideas and memories bubble up from our subconscious. Isn't that what the shrinks and self-help books say?"

Anne let Constance's words settle.

"Do you recall anything you said while under hypnosis?"

"Yes, but what I remember most is a man. I saw him, and I felt so strongly that I knew him."

Constance leaned in with interest. "A man? Did you tell Dr. Weiss about this man?"

"No… I didn't tell her everything I saw. It's hard to explain but, when I was under hypnosis, I felt that I was both in my body and yet out of it, looking on, exploring as if I were someone else. It was hard to speak because I was experiencing so much. And then Dr. Weiss' voice became an intrusion."

Constance slowly rose to her feet. "So who is, or who was, this man?"

"I'm not entirely sure, but I felt so drawn to him. He was in uniform. I don't know what rank, or anything like that, but he had a strong, handsome face, with striking blue eyes. He looked at me with such soft and adoring eyes. His gaze touched my heart. He came toward me and asked if I wanted to dance… And then, dates and times seemed to melt together, and I didn't know where I was, or what happened."

Constance folded her arms. "Did he call you by your name?"

Anne stared with a transcendent expression. "Yes… He called me Anne. And then I knew my name, my complete name."

Constance waited, and her breathing slowed.

Anne's eyes were direct. "My name is Anne Billings."

Constance straightened. "Are you sure?"

"Yes, I'm sure. As soon as the man spoke my first name, my last name was obvious. I knew it, without any doubt."

Constance felt a chill run through her. "Anne... Dr. Weiss told me that when she asked you for the year, you said it was 1942."

Anne lowered her eyes, worried. "Yes, that's right. It was clear to me. Yes, it was October 1942... and then I saw images and faces from other years as well, from 1944, I think."

Constance struggled to summon words to fit the strange conversation. "But you see, Anne, your entire session, what you saw and felt, must have been a dream or a hallucination. Maybe it was a result of the medication you've been taking. And you just said the session scared you and confused you."

Anne sighed. "That's right, it did scare me. It had a peculiar reality about it. That's what I was thinking when I stood outside on that window ledge. I stepped outside to confirm to myself that I wasn't dreaming. When I was under hypnosis, that world—the world I was seeing, smelling and hearing—was more real to me than this world is. That world felt like *my* world, familiar and real, and just out of my reach. I wanted to touch it; pierce it, live in it, but I couldn't. This world seems like a dream, a weird, foggy dream that has no basis in reality."

Anne felt Constance's gaze move across her face.

Anne continued. "And what about the clothes I was wearing when I was found? They were in the style of the 1940s, weren't they? Why is this world so strange and foreign to me, and why do I want to go home to the world I experienced under hypnosis?"

Constance's eyes were flat and directionless. "Well… None of this makes any sense to me, Anne. It just doesn't."

Anne sat up, adjusting the pillows and propping her back against the headboard. "I want to have another session with Dr. Weiss. Can that be arranged?"

Constance glanced away. "No… we decided that she wasn't the right doctor for you."

"I don't understand," Anne said.

"She was upset by the session, Anne. She didn't want to continue. We both agreed we should find another doctor… one more experienced in, well, your kind of mental issue."

Anne's head lowered. "Mental issue? Do you think I'm insane, then?"

"No, Anne, I don't. But I do think you need time to rest and to stop thinking so much. Thinking too much will drive anyone crazy. I can tell you that for sure because that's what happened to me after Ashley was murdered. I nearly thought myself into a nervous breakdown and an early grave."

Anne gave her a sidelong glance. "I don't know if I can stop thinking about it."

Constance nodded. "Okay, well, I wasn't going to tell you, but Dr. Miles is going to call you tonight."

"Dr. Miles. Why?"

"He wants to ask you to dinner, and I think you should accept. You need to get out of here, see something of the City; meet people, do things, go places. It will get your mind off all this. What you need is a distraction and some fun. Jon is a fine man, a dedicated doctor, and a good friend. I hope you will accept his invitation."

Anne kept her eyes on Constance. "I don't know if I'm ready to…"

Constance interrupted. "… Of course you're ready. It's time to get out of your head and out into the world. You're young, pretty, intelligent and oh, so mysterious. Enjoy it. Will you try?"

"I suppose so."

"Good. And now I'm going to leave you. Try to rest for a couple of hours. I'll wake you for dinner."

Constance moved to the windows, pulled the curtains closed and started for the door. She paused before opening it, not looking back toward Anne.

"Anne, can I trust you not to return to that window?"

"Yes, Constance. I promise."

"Perhaps you're taking too much medication. I'll talk to Jon about it when he calls tonight."

"I promise, Constance. Don't worry… but thank you for worrying about me and thank you for everything you've done for me. I'll never be able to thank you enough or pay you back for your many generosities and kindnesses."

Constance turned to face her. "Anne… consider this house your home. Consider me… well, a kind of mother who only wants the best for you. Whatever you need or want, just ask, and I'll make sure you have it."

Anne was touched by Constance's words, but also a bit uncomfortable by the desperate undertone in her voice. It was apparent that Constance was very lonely and determined to give Anne everything she wasn't able to give Ashley.

"You sleep now, Anne. I hired a chef to cook us a delicious dinner tonight, with an exquisite 2005 bottle of Bordeaux: a very good year. Even with your medication, you can have a small glass. It will do you good. Now, the menu is a surprise, but I think you'll like it. Are you allergic to anything?"

Anne smiled faintly with a shrug. "I don't know."

"Well, not to worry. It won't be too far off the beaten path. I hope you'll enjoy it."

"Constance… Do you think I'll ever be able to find myself?"

Constance hesitated. "That's a big question, my dear. I'm still working on that one myself."

CHAPTER 10

"IT FEELS SO GOOD to be out in the fresh air," Anne said, as she and Jon Miles strolled along MacDougal Street in West Greenwich Village.

"Are you cold?" Jon asked.

"A little, but it feels good." Anne was wearing a tan cashmere coat Constance had purchased for her. She turned up the collar and adjusted her red beret so that it was tilted to one side.

"I like the beret. Did I tell you that?" Jon asked.

Anne didn't look at him, but she smiled, pleased. "Yes, as we left Constance's building, when the doorman flagged us a taxi."

"Well, I'm probably going to say it again. I hope that's all right."

"Yes, Dr. Miles. That is quite all right,"

Jon made a face of mock pain. "And please, stop calling me Dr. Miles. Tonight, I am officially and definitely no longer your doctor. Your official doctor is now Dr. Lambert."

"Pardon me. I will try to remember, but I may forget from time to time before I get it right."

"Well, if you do forget, it's okay, as long as you drop the doctor part and just call me Jon or Miles."

Anne glanced up at him, brightly. "Miles... I like that. Yes, may I call you Miles?"

"Of course. That's what my friends called me in college and medical school."

"It suits you. Yes, now, *that* I'll remember."

"Good, and as I said in the taxi, I want you to choose any café or restaurant or even a diner if that strikes your fancy. Oh, and how is your leg? Is the walking too much?"

"No, it feels much better. It will do me good to walk. In fact, didn't you recommend I take walks to strengthen it?"

"Yes, I suppose I did."

Anne took in the crowded street with its yoga studios, shiny pizzerias, quirky clothing shops and beer bars. There were narrow cafés, novelty shops, and a coffee bar with fresh bread, pastry and muffins displayed in the windows.

"I like this street," Anne said. "It's festive. But what is a yoga studio?"

"Well... let's see, it's a place where people come together and do yoga. You know, they put themselves in those pretzel-like poses and chant AUM."

Anne didn't know whether he was serious or making a joke. "Have you done yoga?"

"As a matter of fact, I have. Maybe you should try it, but only after you're fully recovered. For now, let's focus on having dinner."

Anne turned her attention back to the street. "There are so many possibilities. Do you know what I'd really love? A good shepherd's pie and a pot of hot tea. That would be lovely."

Jon was amused. "Shepherd's pie?" Then speaking in an exaggerated English accent he said, "I say, are you British, my dear Anne, or are you British? And are you sure you wouldn't prefer fish and chips?"

Anne cocked an eye at him. "Are you mocking me?"

"Mocking? No, not at all. Having fun, yes."

"Well, actually fish and chips sounds quite lovely as well."

Jon grinned, enjoying himself immensely. "And Constance wanted me to take you to *The White Dove*, one of *the* best and trendiest fine dining establishments in New York. But I told her that since I didn't know your preference, I wanted to do something whimsical. You should have seen her face. 'Whimsical, Jon?' she asked, with great surprise. 'I didn't know you had a whimsical bone in your body.'"

Anne laughed, and Jon continued. "Then, I said, 'Oh yes, Constance. In college, I once dressed up as Count Dracula for Halloween and crashed a sorority party, bursting into their house with a flap of my cape and flashing red eyes. I'd bought a pair of red contacts for dramatic effect. Anyway, I flapped around, baring my white vampire fangs, shouting, 'There is much to be learned from beasts.'"

Anne broke into laughter while crowds flowed around them.

"Well, I do remember who he was. Did you really dress up as Count Dracula?" she asked.

"Yep, I did. And, I have to admit, I loved scaring those screaming girls."

"And I'm sure they *didn't* love it."

"I will say, in all humility, and with the goal of impressing you, Miss Anne Billings, that a few of those young ladies later expressed an interest in dating me. Three gave me their phone numbers."

"And did you date them?"

"Only those who would agree to expose their lovely necks."

Anne laughed again, a high girlish laugh that pleased Jon.

"I can see I'm going to have to hide my neck from you, Doctor… I mean, Miles."

Jon stopped in his tracks, pointing at her, pleased. "Brava! This is a milestone in our relationship."

She came to a stop in front of him. "What do you mean?"

"You have officially called me Miles. And do you know what else, Anne Billings? You are beautiful when you laugh."

"Now you're embarrassing me."

"Okay, Anne, I promise not to compliment you any further, except to say that you are also beautiful when you're not laughing."

She turned her shy eyes from him and pointed to a café. "Let's eat over there. I bet they'll have shepherd's pie."

"Don't bet on it, Anne. To get shepherd's pie, we'd have to find an Irish pub, and then hope for the best."

She relaxed into a friendly smile. "I like the look of the place. Let's try it."

They crossed the street and entered the small, shadowy café, with red and white checkered tablecloths, red, centered globe candles, and soft rock music from the 1960s coming from an overhead speaker.

A hostess dressed in tight jeans, a red blouse and a leather vest greeted them with a distracted "Hello." Her lipstick was bright red, her short red hair spiked, and her large yellow plastic hoop earrings piqued Anne's curiosity.

The hostess led them to the only free two-top table in the back of the room, near the kitchen entry/exit door.

After they'd removed their coats and sat down, they were handed paper menus, and Anne struggled to pull her eyes from the eccentrically dressed girl.

Jon asked if they had shepherd's pie.

"Never heard of it," the hostess said, blandly. "I can give you a dessert menu, if you want."

"No, it's not a dessert. It's a British specialty; an entrée."

"Sorry... We don't have that."

When she was gone, Anne looked at Jon, and a smile came and went. "She's quite colorful, isn't she?"

"Yes... You see all kinds down here. Do you want to go somewhere else?"

"No... this is fine."

"But?"

"I don't know how to explain it exactly, but I feel as though I'm in a dream. Things... people... look so very strange to me. I feel a bit like Alice, as if I've fallen down the rabbit hole."

"And that's just what you need—to be out experiencing new things. It could trigger a memory."

Anne glanced about. "I'm sure I've never been in Greenwich Village before."

"Are you sure you want to stay?"

"Yes..."

"Okay, well, let's examine the menu and see if there's anything that appeals to you."

Anne ordered meatloaf, mashed potatoes, and Brussel sprouts.

Jon decided on the salmon burger with avocado and sweet potato fries, so Anne could taste them.

While Jon sipped a glass of white wine and Anne a ginger ale, he leaned back in his chair and stared at her in the candlelight.

"All right, Anne, this is the part of the evening where I'm supposed to ask you to tell me a little about yourself, or a whole lot about yourself."

She let out a little sigh. "I wish I could."

"But we're going to skip over all that, and instead, I'm going to ask how you like New York."

"There are so many lights and people, so many sounds and tall buildings. It's a little intimidating. Whenever I look out over the city from my twenty-second-floor room, it looks so grand and so bright and so infinite."

"And have you recalled anything else from your session with Dr. Weiss yesterday?"

Anne avoided his eyes. "That was a swift change of subject. It sounds like you have planned this conversation."

Jon made a face of apology. "I'm sorry, Anne. You saw right through me. It's just that I'm concerned and, truth be told, I'd like to help you any way I can."

Anne stared down at the table cloth and picked at it with a fingernail. "Then be honest with me and be my friend."

Jon held up his right hand and performed the three-finger boy scout salute. "Scout's honor, I will be honest, and I will be your friend."

She looked long and fully into his eyes. "Then I will tell you that I have recalled other scenes since the hypnosis with Dr. Weiss."

Jon Miles leaned forward. "Anything significant?"

"I was cycling, that is, in my mind I saw myself cycling and, as I passed Hyde Park, I saw men digging trenches."

"Hyde Park, England?"

"Yes. England. I knew it was England, and it was so clear and so present. And then I saw a leaflet on the street being blown by the wind. I pedaled over to it and picked it up. It said, WHAT TO DO IN CASE OF AN AIR RAID."

Jon narrowed his eyes. "Was this a dream? I mean, were you in bed, asleep?"

"No... I was in my room, standing by the windows, gazing out at the tall buildings and flecks of falling snow. I remembered it clearly, seeing it on the inner screen of my mind, if that makes any sense."

"Yesterday?"

"No. This morning."

Jon dropped his head in a slight nod. "All right. Anything else?"

Anne spoke haltingly. "I became aware of a date. September 3, 1939. It was a Sunday, but I don't know how or why I recalled that..."

"And?"

"I heard a voice coming from a radio and I knew who that voice was. It was Prime Minister Neville Chamberlain. He said... Well, he said we were at war with Germany."

Jon's solemn eyes bored into her. "Germany? And you're sure it was September 3, 1939?"

"Yes... I'm sure. The radio said that a blackout of London would begin in the evening, and we should carry our gas masks everywhere. The announcer said that the underground—that is, the subway, as you call it here—would be used for transport and could not be used for bomb shelters. Petrol would be rationed, as would some food and other things..."

Anne stared off into space and was vaguely aware when their entrées were delivered. When her eyes returned to his, he looked uneasy. "What does it all mean, Miles?"

Jon kept his eyes on her, thinking, evaluating. "Anne... What does this memory mean to you?"

Anne looked beyond him. "What does it mean? I think it's quite simple. It means I must be going insane."

Jon stared down at his salmon burger. "I think it's time we seriously consider other options, Anne, because I don't believe, for a minute, that you are insane."

CHAPTER 11

"HER NAME IS MELLY PASTERNAK, and she's my mother's odd friend," Jon said.

"What do you mean, odd?" Anne asked.

They were in a horse-drawn carriage moving through Central Park, passing the famous Bethesda Fountain, listening to the clop, clop of the horse's hooves. A woolen blanket lay across their laps, and Anne had her beret pulled down over her ears for warmth.

Jon said, "My mother dabbles in occult things: astrology, transcendental meditation and tarot card readings. My father's a doctor, a scientist through and through, so you can imagine how well they got along when I was growing up."

"Opposites attract, don't they?" Anne asked. "Isn't that what they say, although I was never entirely sure who 'they' were."

Jon thought about that. "Yes, I suppose that's right. My father finds my mother baffling, curious and, how should I say this, quite sexy. She finds him stuffy, conservative and beguiling."

"So what were you going to say about Melly Pasternak?" Anne asked.

"Oh yes, well, Melly is a psychic, or a clairvoyant, or whatever the term is for people who are telepathic, who seem to possess what you might call supernatural powers, abilities inexplicable by natural laws."

"Yes, I know the word."

Jon faced her. "Truthfully, I've never bought into the whole occult thing, Anne. I'm telling you that up front. I think it's nothing more than imagination and wishful thinking. But... Melly did once predict I would marry a woman from a wealthy family when I was thirty years old. That happened. She also told my mother—not me—that my wife would not bear any children."

"That was not a sensitive thing to say."

"Yes, well, Melly is not so sensitive. She's direct, honest and... well, my mother swears she is authentic and talented."

Anne stared out the window. "Constance said you are divorced."

"Yes, the marriage lasted less than three years."

"I'm sorry."

"I was, too. It's the old story. She fell in love with another man... an older man, which I suppose is a twist on the old story. Don't women usually fall for the younger guy?"

Anne looked at him, trying to read him, and she thought. *Was he sorry? Was he happy about it?* After a minute's consideration, she decided to be bold and ask.

"Did you love her?"

"Yes, at least I did at first. Then, well, who knows about these things? It's another one of life's little mysteries. But I don't want to talk about me and my boring personal history. Let's keep the conversation on Melly. According to my mother, Melly told her two days after I was married that the marriage wouldn't last, and she even predicted the week the divorce was final."

Anne held his eyes, waiting.

Jon lifted a hand and let it drop. "My mother isn't a liar. She's as truthful as a saint. So, I'm caught somewhere between belief in the occult and disbelief, and I'm still leaning very skeptically against it."

Anne turned to look out at snow flurries dancing across the amber park lights. With a gesture, she said, "Oh, look, it's starting to snow."

Jon peered out. "Yes. According to the weather, we're going to get an inch or two."

"How pretty it is. Snow seems so magical, doesn't it? I mean, how it seems to come from nowhere, and it falls so silently and covers the ground so completely."

"You're a poet, Anne."

She shrugged, turning to him with a frank curiosity. "Do you want me to see Melly Pasternak, Miles?"

He ran a hand through his hair and down his face. "Anne, I have seen people die, and I hate it. I always feel as though I've failed, even though I know we're all going to die someday. I have also seen people almost die and then come back to life. They describe all kinds of experiences, from going to heaven, to meeting long dead family members, to running through fields of beautiful flowers and trees. I have also heard Melly talk about past lives. She claims that in some people, she can actually see a past life."

Anne listened intently. "Is that what you think I saw in my session with Dr. Weiss?"

"I don't know, Anne, but if you're willing, I can arrange for you to meet Melly. It's against my better judgment and my core beliefs, but then again, who knows? Maybe she can help you, and if she can somehow shed some light on what it is you're experiencing, it might be worth a try."

Anne lowered her eyes, assessing his words, probing the possibility. "Where do you think I came from, Miles? Why hasn't anyone come forward to identify me? Why do I feel like a stranger from another world, because this world doesn't seem like home to me?"

Jon stared earnestly. "I don't know, Anne. This morning, I called the detective in charge of your case. They don't have any new information. Nothing."

Anne's eyes slid away from his direct stare. "This afternoon, Constance typed my name into her computer, my full name, Anne Billings. I couldn't believe what I was seeing. There were so many, from all over the world, but none of them were me. I just don't understand."

"Do you want me to set up a meeting with Melly?"

Anne took in a breath, letting it out at once. "I'm so scared, Miles. I'm scared all the time and I'm so sick and tired of being scared. This morning, while I was drifting in and out of sleep, I saw the face of a little boy. He was calling out to me. Reaching for me. I knew him. I knew who he was, but before I could recall his name, I woke up. He was gone, and his name, which had been on the tip of my tongue, was also gone."

When the carriage came to a stop near Fifth Avenue, there was a long moment before either said anything.

Anne finally broke the silence. "Yes, Miles. Yes, please contact Melly Pasternak. Maybe she'll be able to tell me what is happening. I'm desperate."

THAT NIGHT, ANNE COULDN'T SLEEP. She tossed back the comforter and left the bed, walking to the windows. She peered out into the night at the muted lights of the city, while snow flurries drifted, while a wobbling siren below filled her with sudden, mystifying terror. Instinctively, she glanced up into the sky as if anticipating some approaching disaster.

And then she shut her eyes. A movie began to play, projected onto the screen of her inner vision. She was walking along a dirt path with a man beside her; a man dressed in uniform, a pilot's wings pinned above his left breast pocket, and he was wearing an officer's hat.

The sun was warm, the day bright. The path had shrubbery. There were curves and turns past a flower garden, a wrought-iron gate and a pond. There was a public space with wooden benches where a woman sat feeding pigeons; where a young couple sat close, he in uniform. They held hands, their faces somber, their conversation low.

The man beside Anne reached for her hand and held it gently.

"Can you meet me next weekend, Saturday? I'll get another leave."

They walked into a sheltered grove and paused in the shadows. He looked at her with soft, loving eyes. "Did I tell you today that you're the prettiest girl in the world?"

Anne thought him the most handsome and dashing man she'd ever seen, with his lantern jaw and considerable breadth of shoulder.

"This morning, you only said I was the prettiest girl in London," she joked.

He pretended to be stricken. "Did I say that? Forgive me, Anne, I'm just a dumb American from Chicago. This morning I must have been blind. This afternoon, I see you a lot more clearly."

And then he kissed her, a warm, gentle kiss that stirred her desire and left her wanting for more.

As they strolled, Anne felt a loving warmth in her chest that swelled and pulsed. "Of course, I'll meet you next Saturday, First Lieutenant Kenneth Cassidy Taylor."

He looked at her with amusement. "Holy smoke! My full rank and name. You make me sound as important as General Eisenhower."

"Oh, you're much more important than he is," Anne said, with a little laugh. "And you're more handsome, and you're smarter, since you think I'm pretty, and you're, oh, much younger than General Eisenhower."

And then they heard it—the piercing howl of the air raid sirens. They turned their anxious faces skyward, tension and fear twisting Anne into a hard knot.

She saw German bombers approaching, bursting through the high clouds, the angry drone of their engines chewing the air, the bombs already raining down. Anne's heart jumped into her throat, as racing footsteps, honking horns and piercing cries of terror filled the air.

"Come on, Anne," Ken said, seizing her hand and tugging her across the lawn. "Let's get to an air raid shelter. Those Heinkels and Stukas are coming in fast."

CHAPTER 12

The following Saturday, Anne sat in Melly Pasternak's parlor, her hands twisting nervously. In concise, halting words, she recounted her entire story to Melly, who listened attentively, as still as a block of ice, her big, bold eyes not moving.

No one in the room moved. Any detail that Anne overlooked was provided by Jon or Constance.

Melly had a wrinkled, unpleasant face; an old woman's scowling face, with lean features, sharp angles, and high cheekbones. Her tight line of a mouth expressed a permanent "No," and her eyes were crafty, her body thin. Her dress was a patchwork of styles, long to her ankles, covering her arms, the colors black, red and green, with a high lace collar. Her hair was a shiny gray and piled on top of her head, expertly molded into a snug, pugnacious bun.

Anne concluded her story and then felt utterly intimidated and frightened. She was about to shoot up from the heavy Victorian sofa and rush out of the room, certain that Melly was a lunatic who was going to attack her, when, suddenly, Melly's countenance underwent a sudden and drastic transformation. Her face relaxed with a wise smile, and her features softened, revealing depth and clarity in her large, dark eyes.

Constance and Anne had taken a private limousine for the two-hour drive to Hudson, New York. Melly's Victorian house sat on a snakelike road not far from the town, with its mid-century antique shops, old-school diner, upscale brasserie, and lively, contemporary art scene.

Melly's house was an amalgam of decorating styles, mixing glamor with kitsch; mixing bright colors with muted ones; mixing traditional landscape paintings with squiggles, skewed perspectives, distorted shapes and clashing bursts of color.

Constance sat stiffly next to Anne on the sofa, her eyes narrowed, her expression sullen, her arms crossed, as if she were trying to shut out the entire despicable experience.

To Jon, it was clear that Constance had taken an immediate dislike to Melly. Constance stared at Melly with a challenge, like a mother bear ready to protect her cub from a hunter.

Jon stood meekly behind the sofa, his hands in his pockets, his cell phone vibrating every few minutes. He was castigating himself for arranging the meeting. Melly was more eccentric, unpredictable, and intimidating than he'd remembered. Or maybe, as she'd aged, she'd grown even more bizarre.

Melly sat in a tall, austere, high-back chair, her arms resting on the broad wooden arms. When she spoke, she had a slight accent, although, for the life of him, Jon could never figure out what the accent was. Not quite Russian or German or Slavic. Her voice was surprisingly low, sonorous and pleasing to the ears, and Jon had often thought that she would have been a perfect late-night DJ on some jazz radio station.

"My grandfather was Russian," Melly said bluntly, "and he was proud of it. He was a rough, roaring man who was killed in a duel, if you can believe it. My grandmother was a gypsy, and one did not cross her."

Melly held up a warning finger, leaned forward, and waggled it. "No, you did not, ever, cross my grandmother. She performed incantations and curses, and she possessed little trinkets that jingled and jangled in the night whenever she was casting dark spells."

Constance rolled her eyes, fighting a towering impatience.

Melly kept talking. "But she had gifts, didn't she? Yes! Gifts that were inherited from her mother and her grandmother. My own mother did not possess these gifts, nor did she want to. Her nature was mild, dull and distant. My father played the violin and was an excellent musician. He played on the street; he played in restaurants; he played in symphony orchestras. He died playing his violin. When he keeled over on the stage, he was giving a recital in New York, playing the *Violin Sonata No. 7 in C minor* by Ludwig van Beethoven. The circumstances of his death were reported on the second page of *The New York Times*."

Melly fixed Anne with a stare. "Do you know that Beethoven sonata, Ms. Billings?"

Anne gave a little shake of her head.

"No? You should listen to it. You'd like it. It has force, passion and mystery, and that is what I feel about you. I felt it right away, as soon as I looked into your eyes."

Constance cleared her throat, shook her head in annoyance, and looked away toward the fireplace.

Jon began to sweat.

Melly pushed to her feet. "Ms. Billings and I need privacy now. We'll go to my back room. I use it only for my sessions."

"I don't think that's a good idea," Constance said tartly.

Melly was unfazed. "It has nothing to do with ideas, madam, and everything to do with why you came to see me. Since you came all this way, don't you think it is sensible that I spend time alone with Ms. Billings so I can fully scrutinize the young woman, without the interference of the outside? That room is soundproof, and it holds years of energy from my communion with the unseen, mystical worlds."

Constance could feel her blood pressure shoot up, and she was about to speak when Jon jumped in before she could. "Since we're here, Constance, why not let Melly at least examine Anne?"

"I can speak for myself," Anne said, candidly.

Constance shot her a glance. "Are you well enough for this, Anne?"

"We've already been over this, Constance. Yes... and now that we're here, I'd like to see what Mrs. Pasternak has to say."

Melly didn't miss a beat. She extended an arm to Anne. "Come with me, darling, and let us get started. Time and tide are all about us. Let us explore your mystery and see what my guides have to say about it."

After they were gone, Constance boosted herself off the couch and walked to the front picture window. "I don't like the woman, Jon. I wish you'd never mentioned her to Anne. And Melly? What kind of name is Melly, anyway? She's unbalanced, crazy. I can see it in her eyes. I have another therapist ready and waiting to see Anne whenever she says the word."

It hadn't gone unnoticed by Jon that Constance was becoming increasingly protective, controlling and possessive of Anne. He was concerned that she would try to choreograph Anne's every move and decision, for although Anne had a stronger will and personality than he had originally thought, she was weakened by confusion, ready to try anything that might help show her the way.

"I want to take Anne on a cruise to the Greek islands, on my friend, Blake's, private yacht. I called him yesterday. I think it would be the best thing for Anne. A complete change of scenery and culture will help quiet her mind and heal her body."

Jon wanted to ask, "Are you doing this for Anne or for yourself?" But he didn't speak his mind.

"Have you asked Anne?"

"Not yet. I will tonight."

"You haven't asked how our date went a few days ago."

"I asked Anne. She said she had a good time."

"I had a good time, too."

"Good for you, Jon."

"I'm going to ask her out again."

"I don't think that's wise."

"Wise? That's an interesting choice of word."

"You know what I mean."

"No, I don't. What is it with this yoyo change of mind over me and Anne? First you don't want me to see her, then you do, and now once again, you don't."

Constance turned to face him. "I've been thinking things over. I'll admit that, at first, I thought it might be good for Anne to go out with you and have a good time."

Jon spread his hands. "And now?"

"Now, I don't. She's moody, unpredictable, and frightened. I don't think any sort of romantic relationship will be helpful at this point. She's too emotionally vulnerable and confused. What if she forms an attachment?"

"Is that so bad?"

"It could be, if the relationship turns sour or if you find another, less troubled and emotionally damaged woman. You are quite handsome, you know, and handsome men often get bored easily."

Jon shook off the insult and decided to be direct. "Constance, Anne is not Ashley."

Constance's face flushed red; her eyes flared. "How dare you say that to me? What a cheap and awful thing to say."

Jon didn't back down. "You know what I mean, Constance."

She glared at him.

"All I'm saying is this: let Anne explore all the ways she needs to explore. Whatever happened to her, it has deeply traumatized her, and she'll need time and gentle hands to help her along until either her memory returns, or she can reconcile herself with the life she must learn to live in the present."

Constance's expression was cold, with the flat, hard eyes of a competitor. "And you think you're the one to touch her with your gentle hands? They weren't enough for your wife, were they? Otherwise, she wouldn't have run off with another man."

The insult cut him like a knife, and he stood, hurt and wounded. His eyes flashed with rage, and he opened his mouth to attack, but stopped, closed his mouth and looked away. The quiet between them expanded into a pulsing bitterness.

.

CHAPTER 13

Anne rested in a soft, leather recliner, tilted back, her eyes closed. It was a spare room, with a snow-white carpet, bare walls and large amethyst crystals placed in each corner of the room. Navy blue curtains were drawn against natural light; the only illumination came from three, evenly spaced candles in elaborate candlestick holders that sat on the black marble mantel. The trembling flames washed the walls in dancing, shadowy patterns. The room was so quiet that Anne could hear the ringing in her ears.

While Anne waited nervously, Melly sat in a high-backed chair, identical to the one in the parlor. Her eyes were shut; she whispered inaudible words and waved a thin hand in the air, and then reached an arm out, as though something or someone approached.

Anne felt foolish and uncomfortable, sorry she'd agreed to surrender herself to this weird woman. Melly's incessant whispers seemed to go on forever, hovering in the surrounding air. Anne rearranged herself and then folded her hands and placed them on her lap.

Minutes later, she heard Melly's chair creak, and she opened her eyes to see that the woman was standing at the foot of the chair, her face in shadow. Her eyes bulged as she stared in wonder and stern suspicion.

There was a crackling tension in the air, similar to that before an approaching electrical storm and its heavy rains. It was unnerving and palpable. Anne was about to speak up when Melly beat her to it. Her voice had changed. It sounded rusty, strained and faraway, even though the woman was directly in front of her.

"You should have died..." Melly said, her eyes not moving.

Startled, Anne lifted her head, not sure she'd heard correctly. "What did you say?"

Melly leaned in closer, her breathing deep. "Death was all about you... I see that. I see the death and destruction. I hear the cries and the terror bombs falling. Yes. In that bomb blast, the very ether cracked and ripped open. Time and space split open for only a moment, and, in that flash, you were thrust through the opening into a death, into a birth, into another world and another time."

Anne stared, nausea twisting her gut. She rested her head back, trying to relax.

"How can it be?" Melly asked, her face wadded up in anguish, her eyes shifting from side to side. "How?

Anne swallowed.

"I'm asking my guides now," Melly said, a hand reaching out to her right, her fingers wriggling... "So we must wait."

Anne's skin was crawling with goose pimples. She began to shiver, terrified of what Melly might say next.

"There's no answer from them. My guides won't speak to me now. There are secrets, things that should not have happened. An accident distorted time."

Anne waited, her hands gripping either side of the recliner, squeezing so tightly her knuckles were white and her hands ached.

Melly made a little cry of pain and Anne flinched. As if pushed by unseen hands, Melly staggered and blundered back to her chair, sitting heavily. She was mouth-breathing through clenched teeth.

"Tell me... How? Why?" Melly said to the walls, to the ceiling. "We must help this girl. Tell me!"

Anne sat up, her face damp, the hair standing up on the back of her neck. A rush of cold wind whooshed across her face, and it changed the quality of the silence. The air—the wind—seemed alive. The candle flames jumped and flickered.

On impulse, Anne pushed herself out of the chair and started for the door. Melly's voice stopped her.

"Wait!"

Anne stopped, not breathing, her back to Melly. She didn't turn when she heard Melly leave her chair and approach.

When Melly finally spoke, her voice was hoarse and low, as if she were awakening from a deep sleep. "Please sit down, Ms. Billings... Please. Don't leave now. I have some answers. Please stay and hear me out."

It was the word "answers" that kept Anne from reaching for the doorknob. Reluctantly, she returned to the chair and sat on the arm of the recliner, erect as a soldier, fearing what was to come.

Melly came toward Anne with a strange and vivid smile. "My dear... In all my years piercing the veil of the dead and the living, and in all the stories that were told to me by my grandmother, I have never come across such a mystery as yours. How do I tell you what even my guides tried to keep from me? I should not have seen your truth, but it came swiftly, in a racing torrent, before my guides could turn off the flow."

Anne's eyes were locked onto Melly's penetrating gaze, a gaze cast in a deep, glowing wonder, lit by the candlelight.

"Anne... you are out of place and out of time. I have never seen a thing as this and I do not understand it, nor will my guides explain it to me."

Anne did not move. "I don't know what you mean. Out of time and out of place?"

Melly searched for words. "At first, I thought you were experiencing a past life, but you are not. No. What you told me... your memories about the year 1942 and 1944, are not fragments from a past life. The bomb blast that sent you forward in time happened in 1944. My dear one, listen to me carefully and try to understand. It is not a past life you are experiencing, but it is your current life, trapped in another time, 2008."

Anne felt the impact of Melly's words like a physical blow to her heart. She felt faint and floating and frightened to death. She stammered out words. "Wha... What do you mean, trapped?"

"Listen to me, Anne Billings. I saw what happened to you clearly, as if I were watching it on TV. You were caught in an air raid in London in 1944. Yes, that is true. You were holding the hand of your child, your boy, when the bombs began to fall, and you had no time to escape to an air raid shelter."

At the sound of the words, "your boy," Anne felt the truth of it—seeing Tommy's face. It was raw and shattering, and the knifing pain in her heart was excruciating.

Melly continued. "One bomb ripped the boy from your hand. Another exploded close to you. That blast should have killed you, but it didn't. Instead, there was an anomaly in the rippling currents of time that I have no explanation for. Do I speculate that the fates, or God, or whatever you want to call it, made a mistake? Just a tiny little mistake? I don't know."

Anne tried to swallow away a lump but failed. Every nerve in her body was on fire.

Melly continued. "The bomb fractured the air and split open the fabric of time and space at precisely the same moment that you were blown off your feet. You tumbled through one single opening of unstable air—a narrow opening—and then you were tossed into the splashing stream of another time and place, perhaps a parallel stream of time. You were as a leaf blown from a tree, falling into the wrong stream and carried off into the future... into this time of 2008."

Anne listened in an agony, considering the punishing truth of Melly's words. Her deep-drawn breaths did little to stabilize her chaotic mind. It was as if Melly had lit a fuse and it was burning toward dynamite. Anne braced for impact. When the detonation came, a big flash in her mind, all hidden things were poured out in an explosion of bodies, laughter, screams and memories. Anne knew it would either destroy her or heal her.

Her mind blasted awake, the debris of faces and houses and airplanes circling about her like a kid's spinning mobile. She recognized the people and knew their names, their voices, their histories. She saw images play out as if on a movie screen—and they were real events that had happened, and she was in them, animated and alive. Holidays, marriages, newborn babies, funerals, all swiftly came and went. Her son, Tommy, rushed up to her, giggling into a hand, then raced away and disappeared into one of the amethyst crystals.

Melly pressed on, and Anne strained to concentrate.

"Because of this anomaly, your life was spared. You were found, and you were administered better care and medicine than you would have received in 1944, and consequently, you are alive. Alive and marooned in another time and place where you are not supposed to be. Anne... You have died and been reborn. You have time traveled from 1944 to 2008 and survived."

Anne felt the tears blur her vision and roll down her cheeks. "I remember him now. I remember my son, Tommy."

Her head dropped, and she sobbed into her hand. Melly stepped over, offering her a tissue, and while Anne cried into it, Melly gently stroked Anne's hair.

"Cry it all out, my dear. Just let it all come out."

Melly remained at her side, whispering comfort, while the tears poured out of Anne in spasms of anguish.

When the emotion finally began to drain away, Anne sat up, blotting her eyes.

"You'll need time to rest and think," Melly said, soothingly.

Anne struggled to her feet on wobbly legs. As Melly held her hand, she swayed and almost fell, dropping back down into the chair.

"Take it easy, my dear. You've had a shock."

Determined, Anne stood again, but a second wave of cascading memories poured in. The truth, the pain and the loss all came crashing down, scene after scene: her childhood, her parents, her husband, Basil Wilkinson, whose Spitfire had been shot down over the English Channel in August 1940.

She fought her trembling mouth and then gave up as new tears flooded her eyes, her face creased with pain. "Oh, my God. They're all dead. My son, Tommy... My husband, Basil. My parents. Kenneth... They're all dead."

The world began to spin, and white lights swam across her eyes. It was all too much to bear, and Anne wilted. Melly caught her under the arms and strained to lower her down into the chair. With effort, she tilted back the recliner and gently leaned Anne back so that she rested comfortably, her breathing labored, her pulse high, her lips moving in little mumbles of grief.

Melly glanced about, as if seeking help from her invisible guides. "Where have you gone to? Why do you leave now when I need you?"

Melly glanced at the door. She would have to go out and ask for help.

CHAPTER 14

Constance and Jon found Melly in her kitchen, pouring water from a yellow tea kettle into a teapot. Jon entered and sat on a stool at the kitchen island, while Constance stood by the entrance, watching the steam rise from the teapot. She lifted her irritable eyes toward the skylight where late afternoon sun streamed in.

"How is she?" Melly asked.

Constance's mouth was tightly shut. There was much she wanted to say to Melly, but she'd decided to keep it to herself, at least until Anne was well enough to get out and away from the house.

"She's resting well now," Jon said.

He looked at Constance. "I don't think she'll be ready to leave, at least not until tomorrow."

"Don't be ridiculous," Constance said. "Of course we'll leave. She'll wake up in an hour or so and we'll go. The car will be waiting." Melly glanced over but remained silent. Constance had already had one outburst, and Melly did not want to experience another.

"The tea will be ready in five minutes or so. Shall I make some sandwiches? I also have cheese, fresh fruit and crackers."

"I'd love some cheese and fruit," Jon said.

"I'll just have tea," Constance said, crisply.

"Please come in and sit down, Constance," Melly offered.

Constance paused a moment before doing so, sitting across the island from Jon.

"I thought you said you needed to get back to the hospital, Jon," Constance said.

"I called in and got someone else to cover for me. I want to make sure Anne is feeling better."

There was silence until after the tea was poured and Melly had artistically displayed cheese, crackers, fruit and sliced baguette on a cheese plate.

"We can move to the dining room if you think that might be more comfortable," Melly said.

They all agreed they'd stay in the kitchen, and there was no small talk. Constance finally broke the silence. "Why do you still refuse to tell us what you told Anne, Mrs. Pasternak?" she asked curtly.

Melly's voice was calm, but firm. "As I explained earlier, I think Anne should tell you herself when she is recovered and ready to discuss it. I don't feel comfortable telling you, nor do I think it is proper for me to share what I know is a highly painful and personal experience."

Jon was every bit as curious to know what had happened to Anne as Constance was and, in his own way, he was also peeved with Melly for not explaining why Anne had fainted. But he was intrigued. Something dramatic had happened. He knew that fact as soon as he'd rushed into the room and seen Anne lying in the chair, her face damp with perspiration and her color as white as snow. And she kept crying out, "Tommy... Tommy... where are you?"

"I will tell you both this," Melly said, her teacup close to her lips. "She is going to need caring for, and she's going to need patient understanding. I would further suggest that, when she tells you her story, you do not question her, nor share that story with anyone else."

Constance looked away with disgust. "Of course she'll be cared for, and of course I will be patient with her. She'll have the best of care."

They fell into an awkward silence that wasn't broken until Constance saw Anne standing in the doorway, staring. Constance shot up and went to her. Melly lifted her chin curiously, and Jon left his stool and approached, his eyes exploring.

"How are you, Anne?" Constance asked, noticing her sleepy eyes. "You still look pale."

And then Constance saw it, and Jon saw it. They exchanged furtive glances to confirm their observations.

Anne had changed; her face was transformed. Where there had once been meek confusion and sad fatigue, there was now certainty and grim determination.

Melly slowly rose and stood in place, appraising Anne's expression.

Constance was unsure and gently startled. "Anne... What has happened?"

Anne looked first at Constance, then to Jon and then to Melly.

To Melly, she said, "Did you tell them, Mrs. Pasternak?"

Even Anne's voice was changed; it was deeper, stronger and more confident.

Melly shook her head. "No, Anne, I didn't tell them. That's for you to tell or not to tell."

Anne smiled her gratitude. "Thank you. I appreciate that."

"Tell us what?" Constance asked, noticeably uneasy. "What is going on? Why all this dramatic intrigue? Will someone please just tell me what happened in there?"

Jon pretended casualness, but he was worried. "Why don't you sit down, Anne? Have some tea and something to eat."

Without a word, Anne did so. Melly retrieved a cup and saucer from the cupboard and poured her a cup. "It's English Breakfast. I thought you might like it," Melly said, with a private smile.

Anne smiled her reply.

Constance was losing patience. "It's rude to keep this between the two of you."

Anne added milk and sugar to her tea and stirred, avoiding Constance's probing gaze.

"You're right, Constance. You should be told," Anne said. "Jon should be told."

Anne rested her eyes on Melly. "Would you please tell Constance and Miles, Mrs. Pasternak? I don't believe I have sufficiently recovered to... Well, to explain what truly cannot be explained."

Jon Miles returned to his seat, waiting.

Constance did not move, but an eyebrow was arched expectantly, and her expression said, "Get on with it."

Melly sat, offering a tight smile. "I will tell you what transpired, but I will not try to explain it, and I ask that you not interrupt until I have finished. Is that agreed?"

"Whatever," Constance said.

Jon nodded. "Agreed."

"Mrs. Crowne, I suggest you sit down," Melly said. "The truth of Anne's story will not be easy for you to take."

Constance blew out an annoyed breath and sat down next to Anne, who continued to stir her tea. She had yet to take a sip.

When Melly began, she didn't look directly at anyone. She stared into the distance as if entranced, selecting her words carefully, building to the moment when she first pierced the veil of Anne's troubled mind and began to see into her past.

When Melly described Anne and her son, Tommy, walking briskly along the sidewalk, her voice held tenderness. It took on strength and fear as she pointed toward the ceiling, where she witnessed the low rumble of the approaching German bombers.

As the bombs exploded all around her, Melly shrank down, her eyes darting about as if she were desperately searching for shelter. She pointed, her eyes widening in fear and her breath puffing in and out.

Constance sat on the edge of anxiety, struggling to process what she was hearing. Jon stared in utter fascination. Anne continued to stir her tea, her eyes wide open and fixed ahead.

Melly concluded the story, her attention focused inward, her speech coming in fits and starts as she described how Anne had been blown into the air, while death, terror and the chaos of war were all around her.

Constance gave Melly a squinting leer when the woman described how Anne had burst through a ripped fabric of time in 1944 and had dropped onto the grass in Central Park in 2008, injured and close to death.

Melly finished the story with effort, as the energy seemed to have drained from her. Her chin dropped onto her chest, and she inhaled several deep, calming breaths.

Jon looked at Melly with doubt and speculation. He glanced at Anne. She sat in a drooping despondency, the spoon still in her hand, not moving, her eyes glazed with fatigue.

Constance shook her head in slow disbelief, her careful attention on Anne. She reached for her hand and held it. "We need to get you home, Anne. You'll feel so much better there. I'll order us a lavish dinner and, after you eat, you can go straight to bed and sleep for as long as you like. Sleep for an entire week if you want. I'll bring you breakfast in bed every morning. You'll forget all this... this ridiculous fantasy, and we'll move on and start planning your future."

Anne slowly raised her eyes. "You've been so kind to me, Constance. What would I have done without you?"

Constance straightened with pride. "The important thing is that we found each other, and now it's time to return home so you can rest and recover, while you decide what you want to do with your life. Whatever that decision is, Anne, I hope you'll let me be a part of it."

Anne stared, her body filling with anxiety.

Constance patted her hand. "Forgive me for bringing you here. I'm so sorry you had to go through this... this awful experience. It's unforgiveable what this woman has done to you. Completely and utterly unforgiveable."

Melly was too tired to lift her head in protest.

Jon slowly got to his feet, wanting to help in some way, but not knowing what to say or do.

Anne's eyes softened on Constance. "You don't understand, do you, Constance? You and Miles don't understand, and how could you? How could anyone understand it?"

"Understand what, Anne? Tell me. I want to help," Constance said, her head inclined forward. "I'll help you any way I can."

Anne's face took on strength and there was a force in her eyes that Constance had never seen.

"What is it, Anne?"

Anne lowered her eyes. "I want to go home."

"Yes, yes. We'll leave right now."

"I want to go home to England, Constance. I want to return to my life in 1944."

Constance's face fell.

Jon's lips parted in surprise.

Melly's head lifted. "My dear, Anne," she said weakly. "You can't go back. What happened to you was an impossible accident that will never happen again. You must know that. You can never go back to 1944."

In a sudden, swift motion, Anne was on her feet, face determined. "I can go back, and I will go back! I will find a way. You said that it was a mistake, that I shouldn't be here. Well, if it is a mistake, then maybe the fates, or God, or whoever, will find a way to get me back to my own time. My little boy is back there; my life is back there, and I will find a way to return, even if it kills me."

The room filled with an icy, startled silence.

CHAPTER 15

"SHE WON'T TALK TO ME," Constance said, obviously upset. She was stalking back and forth in the living room, while Jon stood watching her, a heaviness all about him.

"She said she doesn't want to talk to anyone, including you, Jon—or Miles—or whatever she calls you. How many times have you phoned her? Six, seven?"

After a considered amount of time he said, "Many times. No, she won't talk to me, either."

Constance brought a worried knuckle to her lips as she paced. "I gave her a laptop and showed her how to use the thing, and she's been in her room for two days, ever since we returned from Hudson, New York. She hardly eats, and I don't think she's sleeping all that much. I suggested she see another doctor, but she won't hear of it. She says she wants to be alone. Then she clams up and says nothing. She just stares out the window. I'm worried sick about her."

Constance stopped pacing and faced Jon. "She's much worse than she was, and I can't shake the conversation we had in the car on the way back home the other day. She just kept repeating some version of 'I know who I am, and I shouldn't be here.' And 'I have to get back home.'"

Constance glared at Jon. "I'll never forgive you for sending her to that crazy woman. Never."

Jon released a long exhalation. "Is that why you asked me over? To keep scolding me?"

He glanced at his watch. "It's nearly seven. I still have rounds to make at the hospital and I haven't eaten since breakfast. I'm here because you said it was important. Okay, so tell me, what is so important, besides what I already know?"

Constance's gaze strayed to the windows, and she forced a change of mood. "There are three reasons I asked you to come. The first... I need support. You're the only person who knows and understands what's going on with Anne. I can't talk to any of my friends, although some have been calling, wanting to meet her."

Constance hesitated. She went to the couch and sat, her thoughts circling.

"Okay, Constance. What are the second and third?" Jon asked.

She didn't look at him. "I've been reading articles on the internet about schizophrenia, and I talked to an old friend of my husband's, Dr. Magnus Richardson. He's a psychiatrist who saw Charles during a time when he was struggling with depression and alcohol. I explained Anne's situation as best I could, and he said he'd be happy to meet and talk with her. I told Anne about my conversation, but she refused to see him. 'No more doctors,' she said."

Constance closed her eyes and pinched the bridge of her nose, taking a pause to gather herself before resuming. "I asked Dr. Richardson directly if he thought Anne was schizophrenic. You know how you doctors are, you never give an opinion until you've performed so many tests that you can bankroll a new yacht."

Jon didn't take the bait and defend himself or his fellow doctors. "But you pressed the good doctor, didn't you, Constance?"

Constance's eyes popped open. "You bet I did. I'm worried sick about Anne. She's not the woman she was. She's really changed."

Jon eased down in a chair opposite Constance. "Of course, it's possible Anne has schizophrenia, or maybe even DID, Dissociative Identity Disorder. That's the new term for multiple personality disorder, in case you didn't know. But I think..."

Constance cut in. "... Yes, Dr. Richardson suggested both conditions as a possibility, but then he stressed that Anne would have to undergo a battery of tests."

Jon leaned forward. "I've also been doing some research. I spoke to a psych doctor and a neuropsychologist at the hospital."

Constance listened, absorbed. "And...?"

"The problem with DID is that it's hard to diagnose and challenging to treat. All they know is that it usually develops in childhood as a result of exposure to severe trauma or abuse. The traumatic experience could start as early as infancy or occur later in childhood, but usually before the age of six. No one is born with DID, and it seems to develop over time."

Constance pondered. "Well, since we don't know anything about Anne's childhood, we can only speculate, can't we?"

Jon continued. "But none of these explain away all the mysteries. We're right back where we were. Why hasn't anyone come forward to identify Anne? Why doesn't she have any identification whatsoever, and why doesn't she pop up anywhere on the internet or social media? At her age, that's nearly impossible. When she was found, why was she wearing those retro clothes and why did she present to the ER with injuries consistent with the trauma of war, including small pieces of shrapnel in her left leg? Under hypnosis with Dr. Weiss, Anne said, without hesitation, that she recalled 1942 and 1944. After Melly recounted her vision of the bombing in London in 1944, Anne corroborated it. She remembered details about her son. All of this points to something other than DID or schizophrenia."

Constance jumped to her feet, made a haughty, dismissive gesture, and walked to the windows, keeping her back to him. "I am never going to believe that Anne Billings has time traveled from 1944. It's preposterous, and it is insane, not to mention impossible. It's the wild imaginings of silly movies and popular novels."

Jon took a sip of the single malt Scotch that Constance had handed him when he'd arrived. He swirled it, the ice clinking against the glass. "What's the third reason you asked me over, Constance?"

She turned back to him, meeting his piercing gaze. Jon watched the changing expressions on Constance's face: worry, anger, and finally resignation. She moved back to the couch and sat, staring down. "I told you about Leon Fogle, didn't I?"

"The computer whiz kid who was using Anne's photo to search the internet, hoping for a photo match?"

"Yes, that's him. He contacted me this afternoon. He said he has information. Definite information. And, as he put it, the data is 'awesome and wild.' He'll be here any minute, between seven and eight."

"Does Anne know he's coming? Did you tell her?"

Constance shook her head. "No. I don't think it's wise. If it's disturbing news, she could have a breakdown."

Jon stared into his glass of amber-colored whiskey, then held it to his nose and inhaled its rich and luscious aromas. "And what about you, Constance? If the truth is awesome and wild, as our computer whiz friend says, will you have a breakdown?"

She aimed her steely eyes at him. "You know me better than that. I can take whatever life throws at me and I will fight back."

NOT LONG AFTER, Leon Fogel came slouching into the living room, bearing a backpack, presenting a sideways smile and his usual tousled hair. Constance introduced him to Jon, who quickly sized him up as a bright, young, and distracted scientist type, who read books on string theory and quantum mechanics, and lived in the worlds of numbers, video games and Shake Shack hamburgers.

Leon shrugged off his backpack, removed his laptop and settled into an elegant chair near the coffee table.

Jon kept his keen eyes on Constance, who was all controlled nerves and blinking eyes, her mouth tight, her jaw tight, her hands squeezed together tightly in her lap.

She cleared her throat. "So what do you have for me, Leon?"

Leon booted up his laptop and logged on. "Well... It's pretty cool... okay, well, maybe not cool, but it's awesome."

Constance relaxed her shoulders. "Yes, Leon, so you said on the phone."

"You remember I told you about my uncle who works for the CIA? They have these powerful computers that can access databases that reach all the way back to the 1940s, and even further."

"I remember, Leon. Please, just tell me what you found."

Leon looked up eagerly. "It helped that you called and told me that Anne's last name was Billings. Well, they plugged in her photo and... it was a wow. There was a match."

Constance's left eye twitched and her mouth moved, but she didn't speak. She couldn't. Jon sat up straight, trying to swallow away a mounting anxiety.

Leon adjusted his glasses. "It was a match to an obscure photo and an article in a local paper in Stratford, England, in 1944. The photo matched Anne Billing's photo that you gave me. It was within a 98.8 percentile, which means it was a definite match."

Jon kept his startled eyes on Constance. She was breathing fast, staring, not seeing anything.

When neither Constance nor Jon commented, Leon continued. "And what is like, wild and really cool, is that Anne Billings worked for a while at Bletchley Park."

Jon took a generous drink of his Scotch, swallowing it slowly, looking down at his shaky hands. "What is that? What is Bletchley Park?"

Leon's smile was laced with the pride of knowledge. "Bletchley Park was the central site for British cryptanalysis during World War Two. It housed the Government Code and Cypher School or (GC&CS), which regularly penetrated the secret communications of the Axis Powers—mostly the German Enigma and Lorenz ciphers."

Jon's eyes cleared. "Yes, of course. Bletchley Park was where the code breakers worked to break the German codes."

"Not all who worked there were code breakers," Leon said. "There were about ten thousand people who worked in the wider Bletchley Park organization, and about eight thousand were women. They worked as administrators, card index compilers, dispatch riders and code-breaking specialists."

Constance still couldn't let the truth in. She opened her mouth to speak but failed to push out any words. She cleared her tight throat and tried again. "What does all this have to do with Anne?"

Leon scratched his head. "Remember when I said the information was awesome and wild? Well, my uncle analyzed Anne's photo and the information he'd collected. He grilled me like I was some criminal or something. He kept asking the same questions over and over. He didn't believe me when I told him about Anne.

He thought I was playing a joke on them. Finally, I said, I think it's obvious. Anne Billings is a time traveler. A real, actual, incarnate time traveler."

Constance shot up and walked aimlessly, her face flushed with anger. "Don't be ridiculous! It's pure and utter nonsense, and I won't hear another word about it."

Leon shrank back a little. "But... there's more."

Constance glowered at him. "What do you mean, more?"

"Go ahead, Leon. Tell us," Jon said.

"I have the article my uncle found, including Anne's 1944 photo, on my laptop. Should I read it?"

Constance went rigid, her features beginning to fall apart. In a kind of trance, she found her way back to the couch and sat.

Jon said, calmly, "Yes, Leon, please read the article."

"It's short. Okay, here goes."

He nosed into the screen. "*Anne Billings, daughter of Nigel and Rose Billings, along with her son, Tommy, were reported missing after a German air raid struck East London Saturday last, killing hundreds and leaving many homeless and wounded. Anne Billing's handbag was found, containing her identification, which included her home address here in Stratford, and an old identity card from Bletchley Park, dated 1943.*"

At that moment, Anne Billings entered, her face impassive and pale, her posture erect. She swept the room with her eyes, her jaw set.

In the stunned silence, no one stirred.

As Anne spoke, she trembled. "Would you like to know what job I held at Bletchley Park? We were sworn to secrecy, but I can tell you now, now that World War Two ended so many years ago. I remember everything as if it were only a few months ago... and, for me, it *was* only months ago, wasn't it?"

CHAPTER 16

Anne looked at Constance and spoke frankly. "Leon is right, Constance. As strange and impossible as it seems, I am a time traveler, and I am very far from my home."

The color drained from Constance's face, and she broke out into a cold sweat. She tried to stand but failed. She tried to speak but failed. Her beliefs and opinions had been smashed, and she felt naked, exposed and wounded, as if she'd been punched in the gut.

Jon's eyebrows shot up in surprise. His eyes widened on Anne as an unnamed terror rose in him. Nothing in his medical training or life experience had prepared him for the stark impossibility of the moment, or for the gnawing dread that paced inside his gut.

Leon removed his glasses and grinned—a mischievous grin of satisfaction.

Anne spoke in a quiet, matter-of-fact voice. "Bletchley Park was a mansion in Buckinghamshire, England. It was home to the British government's Code and Cypher School, where code-breakers cracked the

Nazi's Enigma cypher. The women who work there came from a variety of backgrounds. I was not a code-breaker. My job was simple. I was a card index compiler, a job that called for a focused, detailed mind and long hours of work."

Constance, Jon and Leon sat still as statues, unaware of the rain striking the windows and the howling wind circling the building, making a sound like a wild animal.

Anne continued. "Some of the women were secretarial college graduates, others were from universities, while others came straight from school at the age of fourteen. High society debutantes were among the first brought to Bletchley. They had the best connections, and they were considered the most trustworthy. In the end, it didn't matter so much where we came from. We were all looking for a job that would make a difference to the war effort, so we worked together. I started at Bletchley in 1941 and left in late 1943, when I could no longer tolerate being without my son, Tommy. I'd gone home frequently to see him, but it wasn't enough. Even though my parents were there, and they loved him, he was growing up fast; he was already three years old."

Anne stared into the middle distance, and her eyes said something bleak. "Did my sweet boy, Tommy, die in that air raid, or was he tossed into another time as well? Did he survive the air raid and go looking for his mommy? What happened to him? Where is he? Why have I left him for so long?"

No one spoke, and the silence hurt.

Anne turned her head away, and her eyes spilled tears. "I have to find out, don't I? I've been searching all over that laptop in there. Searching for Tommy. Searching for me. I didn't find anything. I must not be handling the thing just right. We must be in that machine somewhere. I mean, isn't everything, history and libraries and universal knowledge in that box of a thing? Isn't all the information about people for all time in that... little computer?"

Anne's pleading eyes came to Leon. "I heard you read that article. It's about me and Tommy. I'm from Stratford. My parents live there. I heard what you read. It was me, and it was Tommy. You were reading about us and the air raid that somehow blasted me into this time, just as Melly Pasternak said. Can you please use your box or laptop, or whatever you call it, and help me find Tommy?"

Leon twisted up his lips, moving them left and right, while he worked on a thought. "Well, actually, it was the CIA who found you."

"What is this CIA? Can I talk to them? Can they help me find Tommy?"

Constance sat rigid, blunted and dazed by the truth.

Jon drained his glass and held onto it with both hands.

Leon scratched his head, again searching for words. "It's kind of difficult to..."

Constance cut in. "... The CIA will spy on you, Anne," she said in a shaky, fearful voice. "They will watch you."

Leon spoke up. "Well, actually, Mrs. Crowne, CIA officers can't spy on U.S. citizens on American soil. The FBI is the domestic spy agency. The CIA has to operate on foreign soil. They do human intelligence."

"What does that mean?" Jon asked.

Leon continued. "It means they're best at recruiting assets and running agents."

"Okay, what I really want to know is, what exactly does your uncle do for the CIA?" Jon asked.

"He's a CIA officer. He oversees handlers and agents."

"Can he find my son, Tommy?" Anne asked, her face tight with stress. "Can he help me?"

Leon squirmed as he moved his uneasy gaze about the room. "Ms. Billings, my uncle has already started an investigation of you."

Constance jumped up, her eyes hostile. "I will never, ever, let anyone or any agency walk in here and take Anne away. Do you hear me? You tell him that. You tell him! Do you understand! Never. I know senators and congressmen. I will not let this happen."

Leon was stung by the attack. "But... I..."

Jon stood up. "Constance..."

"I don't want to hear it, Jon!" Constance yelled. "Not one word. You stay out of this."

Jon straightened his shoulders. "If you call your senators and congressmen, this whole thing will blow up in your face. There's no telling what will happen to Anne."

"Keep your mouth shut, Jon, do you understand?" Constance raged. "Just shut up about it!"

Anne spoke up, her voice full of force. "I have to get back to England."

Constance stared at her, the rage melting away, replaced by confusion. "England?"

"Yes. When can I go?"

Jon combed a hand through his hair. "Anne, you have no identification. No passport. In this time, you don't exist, at least not on any legal document. You can't leave the country."

Feeling desperate, Anne turned to Leon. "Can this CIA get me what I need? A passport? An ID?"

Leon seemed to shrink into himself, refusing to look at anyone. "My uncle didn't believe me at first. He said I was making everything up. He didn't believe any of it."

"What is your uncle's name, for God's sake?" Constance demanded.

"Alex Fogel."

"But he believes you now?" Jon asked.

Leon shrugged. "I don't know. I mean... he said he was going to do some investigating."

Leon raised his eyes to Jon. "He said he would investigate the police report and Miss Billing's hospital records and... well, whatever else, even though I told him there was nothing else."

Tension and fear pulled Constance's face out of shape into ugliness. Her feelings were strangling her. "This is... well, it's absolutely insane. All of it. It just can't be."

Constance faced Anne, speaking in a breaking voice, a beseeching voice. "Anne, you need to see a doctor. You need to get on medication. None of this is true."

Anne hesitated, then came forward, giving Constance a long, measured look. "I believe I know how you feel, Constance. I have spent the last few days wrapped in a nightmare of thoughts, emotions and images. I had to face things. I had to face myself and I had to face the reality of where I am and what has happened. I don't like any of it, but it doesn't matter. It's true. Constance, it is true."

The atmosphere was charged with a chilly gloom, while rain lashed at the windows.

Jon's temples were pounding, and he had a blurry headache.

Anne continued. "I don't understand how it happened, Constance, but it did happen, just as Mrs. Pasternak said. I shouldn't be here. I should be either dead, or living in 1944 with my son, Tommy, on my way to meet First Lieutenant Kenneth Cassidy Taylor. He's an American, and he flies a bomber... a B-17 bomber, with the American Eighth Air Force. His bomb group is stationed at Ridgewell Aerodrome, in Essex, and sometimes I meet him at Waterloo Station."

For a moment, Anne could make nothing out of Constance's expression. It seemed at once thoughtful and puzzled, angry and sad.

The silence seemed to age her, and it also stole some of the life from Jon. His face was slack, his shoulders sagged forward. "I thought it might be true... but I just couldn't take it in."

Constance looked away. "All right, then. Enough. Enough of this whole miserable and unbelievable thing. I need a drink. Maybe two. Maybe I need to get good and drunk."

She went to the liquor cabinet, reached for a bottle of Scotch and splashed some into a rocks glass. After taking it down in a swallow, she poured another.

"May I have one?" Anne asked.

Constance turned, her thoughts foggy. "Yes, of course..." she said, at a near whisper, her hands shaking as she reached for a glass and poured generously.

Constance handed the glass to Anne and then took her second drink down in a gulp, her eyes hard and staring. "Okay, what in the hell do we do now? Because, Anne, as you British like to say, I am nearly shattered."

Leon meekly raised his hand, like a kid in school asking to go to the bathroom.

"What?" Constance snapped.

"My uncle... I mean, Uncle Alex wanted me to ask Anne if she would meet him someplace."

Constance folded her arms tightly against her chest. "Tell him: hell, no. Absolutely not! Anne is not meeting anyone from the CIA or from any other agency."

Jon said, "He might be able to get her an ID and a passport."

Anne seized on that. "Then I could travel to England. Yes, I will meet him."

She looked at Leon. "Will he help me get to England, Leon?"

Leon's eyes were small and scared. He avoided Constance's burning stare. "I... I don't know. I mean, if he can prove you time traveled, I don't know what he will do."

"I can tell you what he'll do. He'll have her locked up someplace," Constance said, harshly. "Leon, has he told anyone else about this? Have you?"

He shook his head. "No... He wouldn't discuss it with anyone unless he was positive. And I've spoken only to Uncle Alex about it. I'm a professional. I guard people's privacy."

Constance's penetrating eyes pierced him with a warning. "Well, you'd *better* guard Anne's privacy. But are you sure, Leon? Are you telling me the truth?"

"Yes, I am."

Jon went into thought. "Your uncle will learn the truth, won't he, Leon? I mean, he's going to look at all the facts and he will want to learn more, won't he?"

Leon nodded. "Yes. He's good at what he does. He looks at facts, with no overlay of imagination or speculation. If his analysis of the facts leads to something... even something crazy like time travel, he'll go for it."

Constance cursed. "When he does learn the truth, Anne will be prodded and questioned, and God only knows what else."

Anne shook her head, grasping the new, terrible reality. "Of course they will lock me away," she said, anxiety rising. "I haven't been thinking very clearly, have I? I worked at Bletchley. If something like *me* had suddenly just popped in from out of nowhere, the military would have locked me away for untold years while they beat the truth out of me, if they had to. They might have even had me shot against the nearest wall."

Constance slammed her empty glass down and squeezed her hands into fists. "Can we stop this? Just stop it. Anne is not going to meet anyone's uncle from the CIA."

Everyone's eyes stuck to Constance, waiting. Her color had returned, and her eyes were filled with a fierce resolve. "I have friends, who have friends. I'll think of something."

Constance turned her full attention to Anne. "Anne, how is returning to England going to change anything? Do you have a goal, a solution? Have you formed a plan?"

Anne lowered her eyes. "No... But this time is not my home. New York is not my home. It's so fast, and so loud, and filled with things I don't understand. I feel as though I'm lost in a nightmare."

"You will adjust, Anne," Constance said.

"I don't want to adjust, Constance. I want to go home to England."

Constance wanted to reach out and touch Anne. She wanted to make all her pain and confusion go away. "But why, Anne? Everything in England has changed, too. The world of 1944 is gone forever. The world you say you came from will never come back. So what's the point of returning?"

"Because it's my home. Somehow or someway, I feel that if I can get back to England, I might be able to—I don't know—put all the pieces back together and make sense of what happened to me. At the very least, I may be able to find out what happened to Tommy. Constance, he is my son, my little boy. I have to at least try to find out what happened to him. You can understand that, can't you?"

Constance nodded, her eyes softening. "Yes, Anne. I do understand."

Anne sipped her drink. "The East End of London has... I mean, in 1944, it had some of the city's most important dock areas. My Dad worked the docks. It was a hub for imports, and it was used to store critical goods for the war. That's what made it a prime target for those German bombing raids."

Anne turned toward her bedroom. "On that laptop in my room, I read that German bombings left as many as forty-three thousand civilians dead and forty-six thousand injured. From the old photos, I saw that my Mum's and Dad's neighborhood was completely destroyed, as were the row houses where my flat was. Of course, I wouldn't recognize any of it now. As you've said, Constance, it's all changed... been rebuilt. But I don't care. I must go back."

Anne's hands began to shake. She took a long drink of the Scotch, as tears rolled down her cheeks. "I have to go back. I just have to. Won't you please help me? All of you? Please help me get back to England, my home."

CHAPTER 17

Minutes later, Leon stood up, a crafty plot forming in his mind. Anne saw his expression and knew his mind was at work.

"Leon, can you help me?"

Leon tugged on his upper lip. "Okay, as I see it, you have two possible choices. One, you stay here and you meet my uncle."

"That is out of the question," Constance said.

Anne held up a hand to placate her. "Please, let him finish, Constance."

Leon continued. "You meet him, you talk to him and you deny everything. You say something like, you were mugged, but you don't remember what happened because you were hit on the head... or something like that. You say, it was all a big misunderstanding. I'll say, you finally snapped out of it, and you remember everything now, so there's no time travel story. We'll have to refine our stories, but something like that."

"Will he believe you?" Jon asked. "Do you think he'll believe Anne?"

Leon adjusted his glasses, looked toward the ceiling and winced. "Honestly... no. He's smart and experienced. He probably wouldn't believe either one of us. The police report, hospital records, no footprint on social media, and lack of any ID are hard to explain away."

"Okay, well then, what's the second choice, Leon?" Constance asked.

Leon leveled his eyes on Anne. "Anne disappears. Vanishes, and you, Mrs. Crowne, say she left in the middle of the night and you have no idea where she is."

Constance massaged her forehead. "I don't like it."

"It might work, Constance," Jon added.

"Mrs. Crowne, if my uncle believes that Anne has time traveled, he will never give up. I know him. Ms. Billings will be a prisoner in this place. He'll watch your every move. He'll talk to neighbors and friends and people where you shop. Neither of you will have a minute's peace."

"Then I'll call the police on him," Constance said, sharply.

"That won't matter. He'll vanish for a time then reappear, while he continues to trace you and your daily activities."

Leon looked at Anne. "It's best if you disappear, Ms. Billings, until we can get you a passport."

Anne set her half-consumed glass down on the coffee table. "Where would I go?"

"I have a house in the Hamptons," Jon said.

Leon shook his head. "No good. Uncle Alex would find her there in a heartbeat."

"This just infuriates me," Constance said. "Why did you get your uncle involved in this in the first place?"

Before Leon could respond, Constance waved him away, knowing the answer. "Forget it... Just forget it. All right, if your uncle is so clever and he will find Anne at Jon's Hampton's house, then he'll also find her at my houses in Southampton and the Berkshires, right?"

"Yes."

"Where would you suggest we take her then? To a hotel?"

Leon grinned, sheepishly. "I would suggest... my place."

Constance jerked erect. "What?"

Jon glared.

Anne brightened. "Does your uncle ever visit you, Leon?"

He shook his head. "No way... I live on East 119th Street and Third Avenue in Harlem. He'll never come, even though it's a cool neighborhood and I have an amazing two-bedroom apartment. I use one bedroom for my office; the other Ms. Billings can have. It's private and I'm not around that much."

Constance shook her head. "This entire thing is just preposterous. I feel like I'm going out of my mind."

Anne took two tentative steps toward Leon. "You wouldn't mind, Leon?"

"No, not at all."

Anne nodded. "Then I think it's a good idea."

Constance turned away.

Leon shrugged. "Also... I know a guy who can produce a passport. Of course, he's not cheap."

"How is he going to do that?" Jon asked.

Constance crossed her arms, looking at Leon with suspicion and disapproval. "Yes, how?"

Anne's eyes glistened with interest.

Leon shoved his hands into his pockets and hunched his shoulders. "So my friend's friend, who used to work in intelligence, has connections to people who stole blank passports from a supposedly secure diplomatic pouch."

Jon threw up his hands. "What do you mean, people stole them?"

Leon kinked his neck. "These people grabbed blank passports from various embassies and consulates. They're sold on the black market for as much as ten thousand dollars apiece. I know it doesn't sound... well, nice, especially since some have been used by gun runners, drug dealers and terrorists."

Constance shut her eyes. "Oh, my God."

"Okay," Leon said. "If somebody else has a better solution, then I'm fine with it. I'm just throwing it out there."

"What if Anne gets caught?" Jon asked.

"She won't," Leon said. "Only the very best counterfeits make it past airport security, but authentic blank passports, when they're filled out correctly, are really difficult to detect. And anyway, Anne is very pretty, and she doesn't fit any criminal profile. Anne will easily get through airport security. No problem. I'm sure of it. My friend is good and discrete. I'm ninety-nine percent sure Ms. Billings will not be caught, or I wouldn't suggest it."

Constance and Jon traded worried glances.

"Do you have any connections, Constance?" Jon asked. "Somebody who could get Anne a legitimate passport?"

Constance's forehead pinched in thought. "I don't know. I'm afraid questions would be asked, and there's always the danger of an investigation. That might bring the FBI, or who knows. Maybe if I offered enough money. I just don't know. It's a gamble."

"My guy's a sure thing," Leon said. "He can do the passport."

Anne's expression was tense. "Constance, it sounds like it will cost a lot of money."

"I don't give a damn about the money, Anne. I care about you."

Anne's smile was tired. "Then I think we should let Leon call his friend. I think I should... move in with Leon. It may be the only way I can get back home."

Constance was watchful and skeptical. She looked at Jon. "What do you think?"

"I have to be honest. Most of my rattled brain still doesn't believe that Anne time traveled. It's way out of my rational comfort zone."

"Forget your rational brain for a minute, Jon," Constance said. "Anne wants to return to England, and she needs a passport. She needs an identity. Do you trust Leon, yes or no?"

Jon stared into a vague, uncertain distance. He pocketed his hands and curved his shoulders forward. "Will you go with Anne, Constance? I mean, to England?"

"Of course, I'll go with her."

He lifted his forehead and looked at Anne. "Then I guess it's our best hope, isn't it? Anne, are you sure you want to do this?"

"Yes," she said, firmly. "I'll do whatever I have to do to get home so I can try to find out what happened to Tommy."

The decision made, Constance stood anchored like a commanding general ready to bark out orders. She looked at Leon and her narrowed eyes carried a warning. "You better be right about all this, Leon, and you'd better not make any mistakes. I want reports from you every day detailing Anne's welfare and the progress of the passport. Is that clear?"

"Yes, Mrs. Crowne," Leon said, suppressing the urge to salute her.

"All right. Anne will stay with you. Contact your friend and let's get Anne her passport as soon as we can. The quicker we move, the better for all of us. If your uncle is as tenacious and thorough as you say he is, we must act fast. We must get Anne to England swiftly and efficiently."

Leon lifted his hand again, to be recognized.

Constance acknowledged him. "What is it?"

"One more thing. It might help if Dr. Miles issued some kind of medical letter or whatever, stating that Anne is traveling to England to consult with another physician. It's a backup, just in case there's any suspicion at all, not that I think there will be."

"That's not a bad idea," Jon said, and then he added. "Should Anne keep her real name on the passport, or should she change it, just in case your uncle is snooping around?"

"That's a good question," Constance said.

"I don't think it will be a problem," Leon said, turning his gaze on Anne. "Ms. Billings, do you want to change your name for the passport?"

She thought about it. "I don't care. I want whatever will work."

"All right," Leon said.

Constance was brisk and business-like. "All right, let's get moving. Anne, start packing. Leon, contact your friend. Jon, write that letter. I'll pour myself another drink and take two Extra Strength Tylenol. And, if I'm lucky, I won't have a nervous breakdown when your snooping Uncle Alex shows up at my front door."

Leon snapped her a look of surprise.

"I'm not naïve, Leon. If he's half the man you say he is, he'll come, and I'll be ready for him. All right, let's get to it."

CHAPTER 18

Four nerve-wracking days later, Alex Fogel called Constance, speaking to her in a smooth, polite voice. He introduced himself as Leon's uncle and asked if he could arrange a time for them to meet.

"Why?" Constance said, crisply.

"I think you know why, Mrs. Crowne."

"I'm sure I don't. By now, I'm sure Leon has told you that Anne's incredible story of being a time traveler was complete and utter fiction. Frankly, it was nonsense, and I had believed it was nonsense from the beginning."

"Why did you take her in, Mrs. Crowne?"

"Because I wanted to. After the trauma, Anne wasn't well, and she had nowhere else to go. In her medicated, mixed up head, she dreamed up the entire thing. I'm sure Leon has also told you that Anne is no longer staying with me."

"Yes, he did. When did she leave?"

"That is none of your business. Wherever she went, that is *her* business. As I'm sure you also know, she left rather abruptly."

"Have you heard from her?"

"Yes, once. She said she'd left town, and she was staying with a relative."

"Did she say where that relative lives and who the relative is?"

"Look, Mr. Fogel, I have nothing else to say to you. If you call me again, I will call the police."

Alex's voice lightened. "I can assure you I'm not an evil guy, but I am a curious one. Mrs. Crowne, I'd love to buy you dinner. I promise not to be aggressive or rude. If you were in my place, I'm sure you'd have questions. After all, Anne Billings' story is an extraordinary one. I've read the police report, seen her hospital records and spoken to a doctor or two. She had no ID, is on no social media, and the photo Leon gave me to scan made a near-perfect match to an Anne Billings in 1944. It's mystifying, isn't it?"

"Mr. Fogel, thank you for your dinner offer, but I'm busy."

"I didn't mention a date."

"I'm busy, on any date."

There was a pause. "Mrs. Crowne," he said, in a low, even voice. "I'd just like to talk to you about it, that's all. It's clear you're trying to protect Anne Billings, and I admire that, but I don't believe you're going about it the right way."

"I don't really care what you believe, Mr. Fogel, and now I must go. I have an engagement. Don't call me again or, believe me, I *will* call the police. Oh, and I know a senator or two so, if you persist, I will have them contact your superiors."

A DAY LATER, CONSTANCE was in a taxi heading for her hairdresser, frequently glancing back over her shoulder, sure she was being followed. There was something both thrilling and terrifying about it; an adventure she'd never experienced. She decided she liked being "tailed," as the gumshoe detectives in the 1940s movies had called it. Her inner laughter at the absurdity of it all helped to release some of the tension. Glancing about frequently, she didn't see anyone. She'd asked Leon to send her a photo of Alex Fogel, so at least she'd know him if she saw him.

While her hair was being cut and styled, her wary eyes searched the wall of mirrors. She half-expected to see Mr. Fogel, staring back at her from some shadowy corner, but he wasn't, and she wondered if that was the end of it. Would the man just walk away?

Via text, and with pre-arranged coded language, Leon kept Constance up-to-date on Anne's state of mind, as well as the status of the passport. Overall, Anne was fine, but she was anxious and impatient to get the passport and leave for England.

And then the passport began taking longer than any of them had hoped. Leon texted *Friend busy. He said, hope to get to it soon.*

Constance had offered additional funds to expedite the process, but she'd been turned down. Leon added, *"Sorry, can't be rushed. Friend says everybody's a VIP.*

Constance met a friend for lunch at Bistro du Vent, a French-style restaurant just off West 43rd Street. Gladys Mecklenburg was in her sixties, richly dressed and bejeweled, full of talk about the charitable events she'd organized for the Metropolitan Museum of Art and the New York Philharmonic.

"I'm concerned, Constance, very concerned that young people today are not engaged in the arts. Oh, there are some, of course, but by and large, whenever I attend the symphony and look around, more than two-thirds of the audience are over sixty, and some much older than that."

Constance was only half listening, as she distractedly scanned the restaurant, searching for him. At one point, she stiffened, sure she saw Alex Fogel at a table nearby, sitting with an attractive woman who seemed to be purring in her snug designer suit. Yes, that's how she imagined him to be. A man who liked the ladies and, of course, they liked him.

"Are you listening to me, Constance?" Gladys asked, her wine glass raised to her lips.

"I'm so sorry, Gladys. Yes, I'm listening. Yes, and I agree with you about young people today not supporting the arts."

Gladys looked annoyed. "I was talking about Thanksgiving. What are your plans for Christmas? I'm in the midst of inviting close friends, say, twenty or twenty-five, for a Christmas Day luncheon. I'd love it if you could come."

Constance pulled her nervous eyes from the room and focused on Gladys' round, plump face. "Christmas? Well... I haven't even thought of it."

Gladys leaned back, appraising her friend. "Constance, does your obvious distraction have something to do with that young woman you took in?"

123

Constance looked down and sliced into her lamb shank. "She has left."

"Left? Do you mean, she's gone?"

"Yes."

"Well, I think that's for the best."

Constance's eyes flipped up. "For the best? Why is it for the best? I miss her. She's a lovely young woman."

Gladys replaced her wine glass and reached for her fork. "I only meant that you were spending all your time with her. I had difficulty getting you on the phone, much less out to lunch or dinner. Now, don't get me wrong, I understand... what I mean is, I can imagine how you feel."

Constance was in no mood for the conversation. "Gladys, I'm going to leave for England soon. I doubt if I'll be able to come for Christmas."

Gladys put her fork down. "England? Do you have friends there? I've never heard you speak about it."

"Charles and I traveled there several times. He had business there. Anyway, I'll be leaving any day."

Gladys patted her sculpted gray and white hair. "Constance... We have been friends for a long time, and I can tell you, you're just not yourself. Something is wrong. What is it?"

At that moment, Constance's eyes strayed toward the bar, and there he was, Alex Fogel, nursing a mug of beer, watching her.

Constance froze in her chair.

Gladys saw the sudden fear in her eyes. "Constance, what is the matter with you?"

Constance jerked her eyes away from Alex in an effort to gather herself. It was clear he would persist, no matter what she said or did. One way or the other, she would have to face him, and face him she would.

Constance tossed her napkin down. "Gladys, I have to go to the bar and speak to that man."

Gladys glanced about. "What man? What on earth is the matter with you?"

Constance rose and started for the bar.

CHAPTER 19

Constance sat down on the barstool next to Alex, projecting courage and a challenge.

His dark eyes shrewdly inspected her.

"I knew you were following me," she said, with a cold, dry smile.

"I knew you knew, so I thought I'd make myself seen."

Constance was surprised by him. He was an attractive, good-looking man in his early fifties with short, salt-and-pepper hair, masculine features and broad, straight shoulders. The dark suit he wore was stylish; his blue patterned tie was silk; his shirt white; his expression disarming.

"Can I buy you a drink?" he asked, cordially.

"I was drinking wine. I think I'll have a Scotch, neat. Macallan Eighteen. Is that too extravagant for you?"

Alex grinned, ordered the Scotch from the bartender, and then waited to speak until the drink had been delivered and Constance had taken a sip.

"Your lunch guest keeps looking at us," he said.

"Let her... She's an old friend. She'll wait, and she'll want a detailed account of our conversation."

"But you won't tell her."

"It depends."

"You haven't told her, or any of your friends, about Anne, have you, Mrs. Crowne?"

"Yes, I have."

"But not everything."

"I never tell everything."

His dark gaze did not stray from hers. "Mrs. Crowne, this is a delicate and sensitive subject, isn't it? The mystery of Anne Billings. Against my better belief and judgment; against my innate wisdom; and against every normal and rational atom in my body, I believe that Anne Billings has experienced something that no one has ever experienced before, or at least not that we are historically aware of. Oh, yes, I do believe we have been visited by aliens from other worlds; I believe in remote viewing, and out-of-body experiences. I even believe in Santa Claus when my grandkids are around on Christmas day, but I do not believe, and never have believed, in time travel."

Constance held his steely gaze. She lifted her glass in a toast. "Good for you, Mr. Fogel. That makes two of us."

While Constance enjoyed the single malt Scotch, Alex sought a way to break through her stubborn, hard crust of defiance.

"I know you lost your daughter fifteen years ago, Mrs. Crowne."

"I'm sure you do. I'm sure you are very nosy and very thorough."

"Yes, I am. A nurse at the hospital told me that you said Anne was, now let's see, how did she put it?"

Alex glanced up at the ceiling, pulling down the thought. "Yes, you said, and I quote, 'This young woman is a mystery just waiting to be solved.'"

Constance shrugged. "Yes, so? Anne was a mystery until her memory returned. Now there is no mystery and there is nothing to be solved."

Alex glanced away in frustration. "Mrs. Crowne, I just want to talk to her."

"She's gone."

"But you know where she is."

"I don't. She didn't tell me. I think she was afraid that you might show up and throw one hundred questions at her. She wants to be left alone, Mr. Fogel, as do I. I have told you the truth, that Anne was very ill, and she was out of her head when she said those things."

Alex worked hard to maintain his practiced courtesy. "Mrs. Crowne, as soon as I told Leon about the Anne Billings' photo match in that 1944 article in the CIA's database, he jumped up into the air and said, and I quote, 'That is so awesome! She's a time traveler. How cool is that, Uncle Alex? She time traveled from 1944,' end quote. Then he high-fived me."

Constance kept her face tightly under control. "Leon is smart, but he gets overemotional."

"For all of his eccentricities, Mrs. Crowne, Leon is brilliant. He graduated summa cum laude from Princeton, with a double major in mathematics and computer science. I wanted him to come work with me, but he turned me down. He is not the overemotional type. For one brief and startling moment, I believed him."

Constance felt her frosty reserve start to crack. She needed to find a way to shut down the conversation and leave. "So now you believe in time travel?"

"Why don't you just level with me, Mrs. Crowne, and tell me what really happened to Anne Billings? I'm not some evil antagonist. My kids like me and my grandkids adore me. Of course, I shower them with presents and candy, but I like playing Santa Claus."

Constance looked down at the Scotch. "This is very good. I usually drink Glenfiddich. Do you know that the Macallan distillery dates back almost two-hundred years? And the Bank of Scotland has issued banknotes featuring the Macallan stills?"

"No, I didn't."

"My late husband was a single malt Scotch connoisseur. He taught me all sorts of things about Scotch. For instance, Macallan was founded in 1824, I think, and it was one of the first distilleries in Scotland to have a legal license for the manufacturing and selling of alcohol."

Alex set his chin, his eyes growing with irritation. "I hear bagpipes, and I don't like bagpipes."

"Well, I love them, Mr. Fogel. When I hear bagpipes, I want to kiss the first Scotsman I see."

"You're being evasive, Mrs. Crowne. I'm sure the Macallan people would be delighted by your knowledge, but you're wasting it on me. I don't like Scotch."

"Don't tell me," Constance said. "I bet you're a vodka and soda man."

Alex drew back, surprised. "I'm impressed. Yes. That's absolutely correct. How did you know?"

Constance offered an arrogant grin. "Men like you are careful and conservative, and they would never, ever let themselves go. If they did, they might break or, even worse, they might lose control. One can drink vodka and soda all night and wake up in the morning with no hangover whatsoever. Again, it was a tip from my late husband, who, never once during our early marriage, ever let himself lose control, except for the day he married me. Then, our daughter was murdered. After that, the booze got the better of him. But that's a sad story for another time, and another Scotch."

Alex was weary of Constance's delay tactics. "I spoke with Doctor Helena Weiss," he said bluntly.

Constance didn't miss a beat. "Of course you did. She didn't tell you anything, did she? She wouldn't. She's a professional."

"It's what she didn't say that was revealing. I saw it in her eyes. I saw fear, and I saw anger. The kind of anger professionals show when they've come across something they don't understand and it frustrates them, makes them feel insecure, small and inadequate. It's the kind of look that says, 'I don't have an answer for what happened, but I should, because I'm one of the best at what I do. But I don't have an answer and I don't want any part of it.'"

Constance lifted an elegant eyebrow. "My, my, Mr. Fogel. You must be psychic to have seen so much from so little."

He turned from her and drained the last of his beer. "All right, Mrs. Crowne. I won't trouble you any further.

Believe it or not, I know how you feel. I have two daughters. One is practical, level-headed, and a successful lawyer. The other plays the ukulele and sings sad songs in dreary, downtown clubs with her boyfriend, who repairs bicycles for a living. I try not to judge either of them. I love my daughters."

A hint of a smile tugged up the corners of Constance's mouth. "I bet you're a good father."

Alex looked at Constance somberly. "As I'm sure you were a good mother to your daughter, Mrs. Crowne, and I am truly sorry for your loss."

Constance avoided his eyes, wishing he'd stop mentioning her daughter.

Alex reached for the bill, glanced at it and pulled his wallet. He removed a credit card and tossed it down.

While the bartender ran the card, Alex ran a hand along his jawline. "Anne Billings was very fortunate that you came along when you did, Mrs. Crowne. Who knows what would have happened to her. She had no memory, no identification, no family or friends, no home to return to, and she was wearing tattered clothes from the early 1940s. And she speaks in a British accent. You see, Mrs. Crowne, I think that Ms. Billings could tell us things about herself, and about her time travel experience, that we could never imagine. If, and I say if, she did time travel from 1944, then it would prove, as Shakespeare said in *Hamlet*, that 'There are more things in heaven and Earth, Horatio, than are dreamt of in your philosophy.'"

Alex retrieved the credit card from the bartender and replaced it in his wallet. He left the stool and, standing, gave Constance a little courtly bow. "Thank you for talking with me, Mrs. Crowne. I won't follow you or bother you again but, I can assure you, I will keep searching for Anne Billings, and I will eventually find her. What a fine and enlightening day that will be. Good afternoon."

After Alex was gone, Gladys came over.

"What was that all about, Constance?"

Constance heaved out a sigh. "I feel so confused and so low. We are such a bewildering species, Gladys, filled with all kinds of mischief and strangeness, and most of it hidden beneath the surface, nudging us, mocking us."

Gladys stared, bewildered. "What in the world are you talking about, Constance? I've never seen you like this."

Constance lifted her head. Her gaze was direct for a moment, and then it drifted away. "I hope I haven't done the wrong thing. I fear for Anne's life."

CHAPTER 20

On her second day sequestered in Leon's apartment, Anne Billings stood before the full-length mirror, her hair prepped and flattened under a wig cap. With trepidation, she tilted her head slightly forward and slipped on the blonde wig from front to back. Standing erect with her shoulders square, she read her face in the mirror. *Who is this strange person?* she thought.

She turned left and right, patting the wig, adjusting it and frowning. It was shoulder length and layered, with bangs. The wig's natural sheen altered Anne's skin tone, and the overhead track lighting accented her cheekbones, sharpened now because of weight loss.

Leon looked on, pleased. He'd bought it at a shop on West 55th Street. When he'd presented it to her, his face had shined with a boyish pride. "I hope you like it. I thought it might be good to have a disguise."

Anne stared into the mirror, absorbed and uncertain. "I'm not sure, Leon. Do you truly think it's necessary?"

"Well... Maybe. Yeah. I mean, it can't hurt. Right?"

"It makes me look... oh, I don't know, a bit cheeky, I think," Anne said.

"Cheeky? What does that mean?" Leon asked.

"Bold and brazen... a little on the saucy side."

Leon stepped back in admiration. "Well, I think you look awesome, Ms. Billings."

Anne looked at him through the mirror and smiled. "You use that word a lot, Leon. Awesome is such a funny word, but I like it."

Leon stood self-consciously, with a loopy grin. "All right, I'll just say that I think the wig looks nice on you. Okay, you're already pretty and everything, but the wig changes your look and that's what we want, isn't it? I mean, it's not like you're going outside the apartment before we get your passport and you leave for England. But I think it's a good idea in case somebody drops in, or if you have to go out in an emergency. It will be a good disguise."

Anne stared at herself, soberly. "You mean, it's a good disguise if your uncle or one of his mates comes by, or if he happens to spot me in the window. Isn't that right?"

Leon removed, and then replaced, his glasses, adjusting them higher on his nose. It was a habit he'd developed in college whenever he'd spoken to an attractive girl.

He was conscious of doing it, but he wasn't sure why, nor was it calculated. He'd often speculated that it might be some subconscious thing about him wanting to undress the girl. Hence the glasses off. But if he didn't slip the glasses back on, he couldn't see the girl so well. And he loathed contact lenses and the ritual one had to go through to keep them clean. It was the germaphobe in him.

"Yeah... I guess that's right. My uncle is clever and persistent, so it won't hurt to have a disguise."

"I'm not sure I like the sound of that, Leon. All right, then, I'll wear the wig when I'm not in my room."

"I talked to the woman at the store about how to clean it," Leon added. "She said you should wash it when it's dull, over-sprayed, or tangled from too much teasing. It's good to keep it nice and clean, I guess."

Anne studied him, amused. "You like things clean, don't you, Leon? Your place is immaculate."

"Yeah... I'm a little scared of germs. When you know about them and that they're everywhere, well, you know, you get sort of... cleaner."

When Anne had first seen Leon's two-bedroom apartment, she thought it something out of a futuristic magazine she'd seen in the late 1930s. And since she had nothing to compare it with except for Constance's lavish home, Anne assumed that Leon's décor was common for 2008.

The apartment had a spotless, clutter-free, open-plan interior, without any unnecessary decoration or detailing. It was spartan, with track lighting, glossy, polished wood floors, white plastic and glass furniture, and open brick and white-washed walls.

An unexpected tabletop sat between the kitchen and living room, and it functioned as a dining table, kitchen worktop and desk, all in one.

Anne's bed was built into a raised platform, hidden from view by a grid of shelving made of maple wood. A series of drawers for storage were underneath the platform, giving the room a modern, chic look.

It was the glass-top desk holding an Apple laptop that Anne had first been drawn to. It sat facing the bank of windows that looked out onto Third Avenue. Leon had booted it up for her and given her a quick tutorial, and she'd spent hours surfing, initially entranced by the images, the online shopping and the infinite reach of information. But, as had happened when she'd used Constance's laptop, she was unable to take it all in. After a time, she gazed sightlessly, as if hypnotized. Her brain was not wired to such impossible devices, and it made her nauseated, frightened, and edgy.

Leon's bathroom had completely astonished her. It was large, made of white tiles and gray stone, with a glass-enclosed shower, a massive shower head, a wide shower seat, and enough room to accommodate four people.

In her wildest dreams she could have never imagined it, nor was there much in 2008 that she could have imagined: the technology, the skyscrapers, the automobiles, the grinding, awful music, and the casual, almost slovenly fashion.

Leon was no doubt an egghead type, with eccentric ways, odd attire, and hair that refused to be tamed by a comb. He would have fit right in with many of the scientists at Bletchley Park.

Back at the mirror, staring at herself in the blonde wig, Anne said, "Leon, do you clean your own flat?"

Leon looked down. "Yeah..."

She gave a little shake of her head. "Where I come from, no man would ever stoop to clean his own room, let alone his entire flat. It's quite refreshing, actually. Anyway, thank you for purchasing the wig. I feel so useless not having any money. All I can do is keep saying, thank you."

"Hey, no problem," Leon said.

"I'll pay you back once I get settled in London and find a flat and a job."

Leon's eyes came to hers. "Ms. Billings…"

Anne interrupted him. "… Leon, please, stop calling me Ms. Billings. We're nearly the same age and we're friends. Call me Anne."

Leon's hands were restless in his pockets. "Anne… You won't be able to stay in London. You won't be able to prove you're a citizen."

The air seemed to go out of her, and she sagged down into the nearest chair. "My God, of course, Leon," she said, sighing heavily. "I didn't consider that, did I? What a bloody fool I am not to have realized it. Of course, I can't stay in England. But where will I go?"

Leon kept his hopeful eyes on her as she sat in a stupor of discontent. "You can come back to New York. Maybe I can have my guy get you a fake birth certificate, a social security card and a driver's license."

She looked at him with cool, distant eyes. "No… I'll find a way. I have to. You'll help me find a way to stay in England, won't you, Leon? Don't you know people who can help me?"

That pleased Leon, who felt both excited and constrained by Anne's prettiness and mystery. He was captivated by her natural grace and elegance, by her lovely speech and startling blue eyes. Alone with her in his apartment, his attraction had increased, producing goofy grins, clumsy steps, and a distracted mood.

Anne had noticed that in the two days they'd been together in the apartment, Leon had often projected a dreamy infatuation and a sweet bewilderment. It touched her.

Leon didn't have a clue how he could help her, but he didn't want her to know that.

"Yeah, well, I'll do what I can. There's got to be a way, right?"

They stared at each other and Anne thought, *If England has changed the way New York has, what will I do? I'll be lost.*

CHAPTER 21

That evening, Leon left Anne alone while he went shopping. He returned an hour later with two armfuls of groceries that he proudly removed from plastic bags and displayed on the kitchen table. There were exotic cheeses, a freshly baked baguette, delicious French pâtés, Dijon mustard, pickled herring, lox, liverwurst, pastrami, baked ham, grilled vegetables, and bagels, along with a container of cream cheese with chives, fresh fruit and a scrumptiously baked chicken. For dessert, he produced a huge slice of chocolate cake, a slice of apple pie and something she'd never heard of, tiramisu.

The sight of it all overwhelmed her and misted up her eyes. "It is so lovely. Such abundance."

Leon took a few steps back and spread out his hands, dramatically. "Well... there it is. All my favorite food from Max Diamond's Deli."

Anne's eyes expanded as she took it all in. "How is this possible? The food I shared with Constance was wonderful and extravagant, but I haven't seen anything like this."

"I wanted you to have a real New York deli experience," Leon said. "There's nothing in the world like a good New York deli, especially Max Diamond's Deli. Okay, I'll grab a bottle of chilled Chablis, some plates, some spoons and forks, and then let's dig in."

As Anne ate, she savored every flavor, often closing her eyes and humming her delight. "This is jolly good, Leon. It's giving me a weak head."

"Do you like the herring?"

She grinned and lifted her shoulders. "Oh, yes, but I've never had it like this. I love it. It's like a dream. So wonderfully delectable."

Leon topped off her wine as she reached for a slice of a baguette and then spread Dijon mustard and liver pâté on it.

"This is pure heaven, Leon. Absolutely heaven. Thank you for this grand and lovely feast."

"I bet you didn't get anything like this in England back in the 1940s."

"Oh good heavens, no. Never. In England, nearly everything is… that is, it was, rationed. Rationing began in January 1940, when bacon, butter and sugar were rationed. By 1942, so were meat, milk, cheese, eggs and cooking fat. In 1944, the greengrocer down the street had very little of what he'd once had. It was so sad. It makes me feel guilty that I'm having this great feast while my people had so little."

Anne turned reflective. "I remember in the mid-1930s, my Mum and I used to go to Walton's. That was the local greengrocer. The potatoes were weighed out for each customer using the 'balance' type of scales, with heavy weights on one side and a large, dusty scoop on the other. I doubt whether you have anything like that now. The door of Walton's was always open, and it was drafty inside, with so many earthy scents. It was scruffy, too, because the potatoes, carrots and other vegetables came straight from the ground, unwashed and unbagged, stored in rough wooden crates. I remember seeing layers of dust covering everything. I don't think you would like that, Leon... all that dust."

Leon swallowed, reached for his wine and took a sip. "It all sounds so... well, so simple and natural compared to everything today."

"Yes, I suppose it was simple."

Leon wiped his mouth with a white paper napkin. "Anne... I hope you don't think I'm being too rude or anything, but... you talk about your boy, Tommy, and an American pilot you were in love with, but you've never said who Tommy's father was."

Anne's eyes clouded over, and she stopped eating.

"You don't have to answer if you don't want to, Anne," Leon said, quickly. "Just forget I said anything about it."

Anne looked at Leon and gave him a sad, bleak smile. "It's okay... Are you familiar with what happened to Britain in the summer of 1940?"

"Yeah... I looked it up the other day. It was called the Battle of Britain."

"That's right. In July 1940, the Germans began their first in a long series of bombing raids against us. It lasted three and a half months. Germany's Luftwaffe conducted thousands of bombing runs, attacking British military and civilian targets all across England. To fight off the bombers, Fighter Command employed squadrons of heavily armed fighter planes, the Hurricane and the Spitfire."

Anne sat back. "Well, you said you read about it, so I don't need to tell you what happened."

Leon said, "What really fascinated me was the Dowding System—named for the Fighter Command's Commander-in-Chief, Sir Hugh Dowding. They used radar, which was really cool and a new technology at the time, plus ground defenses and aircraft defense. For its time, it was awesome."

Anne nodded. "Yes... we were very proud of that. We were very proud of our fighter pilots. They saved us from a German invasion that surely would have come."

Anne fell into silence, staring. "I was married when I was twenty years old. I married a pilot, Basil Wilkinson."

Leon felt a twinge of jealousy, but he hid it. He'd never been able to talk to a girl like Anne for more than a few minutes. Being with her, eating with her, talking with her, all elevated and excited him. He felt bathed in a kind of male glory.

"That was young to get married, wasn't it?"

"Maybe... The war was about to begin, so we married earlier than we'd originally planned. And then the war started for real, and Basil flew his Spitfire against the German air machine."

Anne's voice drifted away.

"So, what happened to him?"

Her gaze was unfocused and bereft. "In August 1940, he and three of his friends were all killed in the space of twenty-four hours."

Leon lowered his head. "Oh… Wow. I'm sorry, Anne."

She nodded, staring vacantly. "After we heard the news about our men, we girls, Nancy, Rose, Trish and I, went to church and linked arms. We prayed and we cried, and we knew we'd never be the same. We'd lost our men… our good and brave men, who had been with us only two days before. But that's the way it was. I couldn't comprehend it. I knew all those pilots. Basil was from a fine family in Henley-in-Arden, Warwickshire. His mother was shattered, and she took to her bed. Her mind was never the same. I wonder what finally happened to her. I wonder what happened to them all, the girls and the families. No doubt they passed away long ago."

"So you changed your name back to Billings from Wilkinson?"

"Not at first… But then my Dad said I should. He said I had to move on and start again, and I loved my Dad. He's a good sort… or was…"

Leon sought to lighten the heavy mood. "And you said you were seeing an American bomber pilot, didn't you?"

Anne looked up, ready to clarify the situation. "Yes, but that was in 1944, almost four years after Basil's death."

She laughed a little. "I seem to fall in love with pilots, don't I? Anyway, on the laptop in my bedroom, I tried to find him, First Lieutenant Kenneth Taylor, but I couldn't. I'm not so good with that computer, I think."

They sat quietly for a time before Anne said, "Maybe I don't want to know what happened to him. He still had ten missions to fly over Germany."

Anne took a sip of her wine. "You can imagine, Leon, how utterly stunned I was when I read on that laptop that the war ended in 1945 with the defeat of the Germans. In 1944, I believed the war would last many more years. We thought it would never end. It was such a relief and a comfort to know that the Allies won, that Hitler died with a bullet to his head and that many of the vile men who followed him fled or were executed."

Anne's breathing slowed and deepened. "And then I read about those atomic bombs that were dropped on Japan. It nearly took the life from me. I couldn't grasp it. One bomb killing so many people is just..." Her voice fell away.

"I can't imagine those times," Leon said. "It's so cool that you were there, living it."

She looked at him with a blank, entranced expression. "Was I there? Yes, I suppose I was."

Anne pushed her chair back and stood up, massaging her forehead. "My mind is such a muddle. I don't know where my home is or where I should be. All my people, my family and friends, are gone... dead. And then there's Tommy. He is such a prince of a little boy. I suppose I should say, he was... but I can't. I called him my royalty boy because he had such a handsome face, with the proud nose and red cheeks of a royal."

Anne smiled longingly. "I had hold of his hand when the bombs fell. I held his hand so tightly..."

Grief took her again, and she wept into her hand. "I'm so sorry, Leon. I'm just a daft woman right now who wants to know what happened. For God's sake, what happened to my royalty boy, Tommy?"

Leon wanted to say something wise; something comforting. "We'll get you back to England, Anne. That's a promise. Maybe once you're back there, I don't know, maybe something will happen. Maybe an idea will come, or maybe somehow you'll be shown what you should do."

Anne's eyes held shiny tears. "That is such a kind thing to say, Leon. Thank you."

She eased back down into the chair. "At night, when I can't sleep, I think maybe I was sent to this time for a reason but, for the life of me, I don't know what that reason is. And right now, I don't care. I just want to go back to my own time and to my little boy."

CHAPTER 22

A day later, Anne was sitting in a Starbucks, two blocks from Leon's apartment. She was sipping a latte; her back to the room, a copy of *The New York Times* spread out before her on the marble tabletop.

That morning, Leon had knocked on her bedroom door and told her that the passport would be ready in just two more days. Then he'd left to meet clients.

Just the thought of returning to England had set her on edge, but she was determined to go. She felt a strength flowing through her she'd never known was there, and because of that boiling strength, she couldn't tolerate being alone, trapped in that apartment, waiting. She had to escape, if only for an hour or so. So she'd donned the blonde wig, applied light makeup and dressed in jeans and a white sweater. Constance had selected Anne's designer shearling lamb coat. It was stylish and warm, and it had cost a fortune.

Anne had entered the lobby of the apartment building cautiously, pausing at the front glass doors to glance up and down the streets. Seeing nothing suspicious, with no dodgy characters hanging about, she started off, finding Starbucks and ducking inside.

Constance had given Anne a credit card, instructing her how to use it, saying, "Buy anything that appeals to you and don't worry about the cost."

Well, of course, Anne would worry about the cost, and she hadn't planned to use the credit card at all. Upon seeing the prices for everything from food to clothes, she'd been shocked, wondering how anyone could live paying such high prices. Paying over a dollar for a cup of coffee seemed absurd.

At her table, away from the windows, it had taken Anne twenty minutes before she could relax enough to take in the room and the people who occupied the nearby tables. Her self-consciousness swiftly vanished. Except for a stout, middle-aged man who had given her a lusty once-over, no one else had even noticed her.

A quick look around revealed that she was the only one not preoccupied with a laptop, a cell phone or a tablet. It continued to baffle her as to why nearly everyone preferred to stare hypnotically into a screen, instead of engaging with the people standing in the line or seated at tables.

Most of them were oblivious to everything and everyone around them. She recognized the convenience and the amazing scale of the internet but, to her, an outsider, modern technology created a bubble around people that cut them off from the world. It was a strange kind of floating alienation that she'd never experienced, and she found it disturbing.

It increased her homesickness, and she longed for her own time, for her friendly neighbors and family, for the local shops and the proprietors whom she knew by first name. How would she ever adapt to this time, to this world?

She was reading an article about the global fears of a recession when she sensed someone standing close behind her. With a racing pulse, she gathered her courage, slowly turning her head. She didn't gasp, but her breath stopped.

On his cell phone, Leon had shown her photos of his Uncle Alex, and that's who stood looking down at her.

"Don't be frightened, Ms. Billings," he said in a calm voice. "I'm not here to harm you in any way."

Anne kept her round, frightened eyes on him. He had a powerful force in his eyes and a stare that held purpose. He unbuttoned the top button on his wool peacoat and then removed his black ski cap, running a hand across his short, gray hair.

Her blood ran cold. She was trapped. There was nowhere to run where he couldn't stop her.

Alex rubbed his gloveless hands together, hoping to disarm her. "It's cold out there, isn't it? I always forget how cold it can get in December."

Anne's chest tightened in alarm.

He made a gesture toward the empty chair across from her. "May I join you?"

She swallowed but didn't speak.

"I promise I won't take much of your time. I just want to, as you Brits like to say, chat a bit."

Anne lowered her eyes and her voice, and she reached for her purse. "I was just leaving."

"Then can I walk with you?"

She couldn't force any words beyond her lips. Was it safer to stay, or to leave and walk? Did he have a gun? Was a car waiting for her outside? Anne's mind and body locked up. She couldn't think. She wanted to scream, but that would create a scene and bring the police. She had no identification yet.

Alex's voice softened. "I just want to ask you a few questions, Ms. Billings. That's all. Please."

Alex saw the wild fear in her eyes. She was like a trapped animal, frantic to find an escape. He decided to chance it and sit. He rounded the table and gently lowered himself in the chair opposite her, hoping she wouldn't make a run for it.

"Would you like another coffee? Something to eat?"

She shook her head, her eyes averted.

"Have you had lunch? We could go somewhere. There's a couple of cafes close by."

Again, she shook her head.

Alex released the buttons on his coat and sat back, appraising her new look. "Ms. Billings, the blonde wig is very becoming."

She wouldn't look at him and, when she spoke, her voice quivered. "It didn't do its proper job, did it?"

Alex smiled. "Leon is head-smart. Not street-smart. Not smart in his gut. I'm very fond of him, and he has a brilliant mind for numbers and logical processes, a good left-brain guy. Did you know that he's got two sisters, both younger, and they look up to him, even if they think he's a bit out there, and a definite clean freak?"

"Out there?" Anne asked, not understanding the expression.

"'Out there' means different, unique or eccentric."

Anne nodded. "He's been kind and generous to me."

"I'd say he's smitten. You are a very pretty woman, Ms. Billings."

Anne reached for her paper cup and took a sip of the cold latte, uncomfortable with his words. She didn't want to be told she was pretty by this man. She didn't trust him, sensing cold calculations going on behind those dark eyes.

"I know the way Leon thinks," Alex said. "I was sure he'd suggest you stay in his apartment, thinking it was the perfect hideout. I'm a little surprised that Constance Crowne agreed but, then again, she knew I would drop by her place and want to speak with you. I also know the awful thing that happened to her daughter, and it's understandable why she has taken you under her wing."

Anne was already weary of his talk. She looked at him boldly, although her heart was jumping around in her chest. "What do you want?"

His gaze was acute and sharp. "All right, I'll be direct. I'd like to interview you, formally, and then I'd like to take that interview to my superiors and get the nod to continue to work with you. Even with the interview, I'm not sure my boss would believe me, but I'd like to try. Then I could put more resources on it."

"Resources on it? The *it* is me, I presume?"

Alex didn't waver. "The *it* refers to your remarkable experience and our further investigation into that experience."

"I have nothing to say."

"I believe you have a lot to say, and I'd love to hear every little part of it, in detail."

"I want to be left alone. Now, will you please leave me in peace?"

Alex leaned forward, excitement making his face young and thrilled. He lowered his voice. "I saw the truth of it in Leon's eyes. That is, the truth of what happened to you. When I showed Leon that newspaper clipping, with your photo and the article from 1944, he turned white. Then the excitement grew in him until he literally shouted for joy and jumped up into the air. Leon is not the emotional type. He's anything but."

Anne glanced about, searching for an escape. Could she leap up and bolt away? But where would she go? She couldn't return to Leon's apartment now that Alex was onto them, and returning to Constance's townhouse was out of the question. Anne didn't want to put Constance in any danger. And Alex would easily find her if she went to stay with Dr. Jon Miles.

She was trapped. The man sitting across from her worked for a secret government agency and she knew all too well what that meant.

Anne's left leg began to twitch and hurt, aggravated by the distressing conversation. The memory of the shrapnel wounds seemed fresh and burning, and nerves beat away at her.

"Ms. Billings, I was still not so easily convinced that you had time traveled, or jumped through time, or slipped through time, or whatever you want to call it. But seeing you here, sitting across from me, I observe that there is something—how do I say it? Something ineffable about you. Your gestures, the way you carry yourself... your..." he glanced up at the ceiling, searching for the right word. "Your overall quality and, for lack of better words, your presentation to the world. I watched you carefully as you left the apartment and walked here. It's as though you're not quite synced to this time; as though part of you is here, but another part of you is not."

Anne looked at him with pale despair.

He continued. "Ms. Billings, I believe that you have had an exceptional experience; a rare and extraordinary encounter with something so mysterious that most people would never consider it as possible. But I believe it. I believe you have traveled in time. Think of it. You'll be examined and interviewed and written about. It will be top secret, of course, but with your cooperation, you could very well change the way we perceive and experience the world. To put it dramatically, you are like an alien from another planet and I want to learn from you as much as I can."

Alex watched curiously as Anne struggled to her feet.

An agony ran up her legs into her stomach, striking her heart. Her head pounded, and she fought to breathe.

Alex said, "Ms. Billings, please sit down. You don't look well."

She faltered, then sat limply down, feeling defeated. As she struggled to recover, she stared hard at him, absorbing the horror of his words.

"Don't be frightened, Ms. Billings. As I said, you will not be harmed. You will be celebrated."

He stared with a pleased anticipation.

Anne's breath came out in shallow puffs. "Mr. Fogel, despite what Leon may think or what you believe, I am not who or what you think I am, and I wish to be left alone. Now, I beg of you. Leave me alone. Please, leave me in peace."

Alex kept his steady eyes on her. "No, Ms. Billings. I will not."

CHAPTER 23

Anne felt pinned to her chair by Alex's unremitting gaze. She fought to control herself. She had to. Panic wouldn't help. As a chill gushed through her and the sounds around her were swallowed up, she sought to quiet her mind.

Alex leaned forward, folding his hands on the tabletop. "I want to tell you a little story, Ms. Billings. Perhaps you've even heard of it. It's a true story entitled *The Vanishing Heiress.* It's about the disappearance of Dorothy Arnold, a New York socialite, who vanished here in New York in the middle of the day in 1910 and was never seen again. To this day, there is still much debate as to what happened to her. When I saw the newspaper clipping from 1944 with your photo and your name, I recalled Miss Arnold's story and I pulled it up on the internet and reviewed it.

"She was a twenty-five-year-old woman from a family of wealth and status, descended from the Mayflower. It was reported that she was funny and smart. Her ambition was to be a successful author. Her uncle was a United States Supreme Court justice, and her father was a graduate of Harvard, a cosmetics and perfume importer.

"On December 12, 1910, Miss Arnold went for a walk. Her mother wanted to accompany her, but Miss Arnold declined her mother's company. Miss Arnold was dressed fashionably and, even though it was a cold day, she walked many blocks to Fifth Avenue. On the way, she passed people she knew and stopped to talk. She bought candy from a store owner she knew and was friendly with. The people she'd spoken to said she was upbeat and happy.

"She entered Brentano's bookshop on Fifth Avenue and 27th Street, bought a book on sketching, and then left. She ran into yet another friend and they had a brief conversation, but nothing of any consequence. Miss Arnold then told her friend that she was going for a walk in Central Park. The friend stated that Miss Arnold was well and happy."

Alex narrowed his eyes on Anne. "And then, just like that, Miss Arnold was never seen nor heard from again."

Anne waited, her gaze steady. "I assume there's more to your story, sir?"

"Yes. Theories, stories and speculation ran rampant. One concerned a lover, someone she'd been fond of and even romantic with. The theory was, perhaps she had run off with him, even eloped. But at the time, the man was with his parents in Italy. He posted newspaper ads asking her to contact him, but she never did. There was a theory that she committed suicide, but everyone she'd met that day stated she was happy and not depressed in the least. There was no suicide note, an oddity, given that she wanted to be a writer, and her body was never found. There was a theory about a kidnapping in Central Park that was purported by Miss Arnold's father, but nothing ever came of it. There was simply no evidence.

"At first, her parents wanted to avoid a public scandal so, rather than call the police, they contacted the family lawyer. He searched Miss Arnold's room and possessions but found nothing the least bit suspicious. Then he searched every morgue, hospital, and ship port for the missing heiress but turned up nothing. Next, the family contacted the Pinkerton Detective Agency.

"The Pinkertons posted Miss Arnold as a disappearance, and they circulated her photo to police departments across the country, along with a one-thousand-dollar reward, a lot of money in 1910, hoping that someone would come forward with information or evidence."

Alex straightened up, his eyes still leveled on Anne. "To this day, no one has ever learned what happened to Miss Dorothy Arnold. Over the next decade, her parents spent a fortune trying to find their daughter, but she was never found, and the mystery has never been solved."

The story had bought Anne some time. It allowed her to gather herself and still her mind. Although the story was an interesting one, Anne focused all her thoughts on how she could break out of the trap she was in. "So what are you saying, Mr. Fogel?"

Alex inhaled a breath and let it out slowly. "There are other stories similar to that one, Ms. Billings, where people have disappeared, or they have found themselves in a future time from the one they left. Like you, Ms. Billings, I believe that Miss Dorothy Arnold stumbled upon a weird phenomenon; perhaps it was a burst of a mysterious wind that carried her away; a fallen tree branch that struck her; or perhaps a hidden doorway that hurled her into the future or the past, and she was never heard from again, at least not in 1910."

Anne's head was pounding as she sought a solution for her predicament.

"Now, as to your disappearance in 1944, Ms. Billings, according to what Leon told me, you were caught in an air raid, unable to escape to an air raid shelter. I believe that a five-hundred-pound bomb, dropped by one of those German Heinkel bombers, exploded near you and then somehow, someway, it blasted you into the future."

Alex reached into his coat pocket for his Blackberry. He quickly scanned it, purposely letting Anne sit in an uncomfortable silence. By the time he replaced his phone, Anne was surprised by a memory; by the fragment of an old conversation that had taken place at Bletchley Park. A conversation she'd had with Roland Richards and Anne's good friend at Bletchley, Harriet Taylor.

Roland worked at the Whaddon Hall facility used by communication staff from the UK's Special Intelligence Service (SIS), also known as MI6, from 1939 to 1945. He was friendly with Harriet Taylor and, in fact, they were secretly having a romantic relationship. Harriet worked as a code-breaker at Bletchley.

The three of them were standing outside on a coffee break on a warm spring day in 1941. Anne was new to Bletchley, and Roland and Harriet were talking shop. It was Harriet who explained to Anne how the German messages were obtained by the 'Y' Service, a chain of wireless intercept stations across Britain and in a number of countries overseas.

Harriet said, "Bletchley decrypts the messages, Anne, and then the contents have to be analyzed. After interception, the encrypted messages are taken down on paper and sent to Bletchley by motorcycle or teleprinter. The final step in the code-breaking process is to send the resulting top-secret intelligence to the relevant people."

But it was what Roland had said that was relevant to her situation. He'd said a spy had returned from Germany, and he'd nearly been caught by two local German sympathizers.

"He managed to save himself because he remained unruffled," Roland had said. "All an act, of course. The chap was bloody terrified. Nonetheless, the old boy told the men that he would cooperate any way he could, and he would jolly well be happy to do so, although he didn't say 'jolly' because he was speaking in German. Anyway, when he had his captor's absolute attention, he told them bits and nobs about his own mission, just enough to make his story believable, mind you—just enough so they could check him out. He gave them some names—fellow Brits who'd been recently captured by the Gestapo. Anyway, then he told them he was a double agent, working for the Germans against the British. With that, the chap was taken to the nearest French café and bought a cognac, just as pretty as you please.

"Moral of the story? Stay calm, distract, and appear to cooperate."

Alex trained his gaze on Anne. "Are you still with me, Anne? You seem far away... Perhaps in 1944?"

She jolted back to the present. "Yes... I'm here. "

"Ms. Billings, there's no need to be alarmed in any way. No one is going to harm you. On the contrary, you'll be treated with the utmost respect and professionalism. I personally guarantee it. Now, I know you've been through hell and back. I understand that, and we will see that you are cared for in every way. If you need anything at all, just ask."

Anne lowered her head, swiftly forming a plan. When she lifted her eyes, she'd regained her composure. "I want to return to my home, my true home in 1944."

Alex smiled, pleased that she was coming around, admitting she had time traveled. That was a good first step.

"Ms. Billings, it won't do any good to return to England. That air raid, and the German bomb that exploded and brought you here, cannot be repeated. You can never go back to 1944. For whatever reason, fate has put you here in 2008 to live out the rest of your life. You can do more for the human race here and now. After we have completed our investigation, then, if you want to return to England to live, I'll personally see to it."

Anne was certain the investigation would take months, maybe years. She was not going to wait that long. And anyway, could she trust these people? Anything could happen. What if they decided it was too risky to release her out into the world to tell her story to scientists and reporters? It was more likely she'd be hidden away in some godforsaken part of the world and never heard from again.

Alex droned on, and she was tired of hearing his voice. "Your knowledge of the past, the people you met… could change our entire way of looking at history.

By the way, did you tell Leon that you met Prime Minister Churchill and the legendary Alan Turing?"

Anne offered an enigmatic smile. "Yes... I met Prime Minister Churchill, and I knew Mr. Turing quite well."

Alex's face came alive, and his eyes swelled with brightness. "That's remarkable. Just damned remarkable!"

Anne gulped down nerves. "Mr. Fogel..."

"Please call me Alex. We're not so formal in this time."

"All right then, Alex. If I agree to all this business, well... I'm not quite sure how to put it, but will I be paid?"

"If I get approval. Yes, of course."

Anne wanted to sound convincing, and she was certain that if she asked for a lot of money, she would appear to be serious about cooperating. "Alex... since I can't return to my true home, and since I'm in a strange and very foreign world, I would want a sizeable amount of money, and I think I would be worth it."

Alex considered her words, inspecting each one. Was she really so mercenary or was she working an angle?

Alex stood up. "Would you mind if we walked and talked, Ms. Billings?"

CHAPTER 24

After leaving Alex, Anne walked for a time until she grew cold, and then she waved down a yellow cab at West 106th Street, instructing the driver to take her to The Metropolitan Museum of Art on Fifth Avenue. It was time to visit the area around the famous Egyptian obelisk in Central Park, where she'd been found; the place she'd appeared after time traveling.

Constance had offered to take her there days before, but Anne had refused, feeling frightened. Now she was ready, and she wanted to see it. Maybe it held secrets. Perhaps if she walked the path, searching the area, she might receive some fresh illumination. It might shake loose an image or a memory. She even entertained the wild possibility that she might find an invisible doorway or a time portal that would send her back to 1944. She'd read about those on the internet.

Anne had left Alex about twenty minutes before, declining a ride, not wanting to spend another minute with the man. It wasn't that he'd made any romantic overtures or been insulting. On the contrary, Alex Fogel had been the perfect gentleman, the ultimate professional.

For her part, she'd managed to keep herself together and project an air of renewed strength, leaving him with the impression that, even though her mind wasn't completely made up, she was open to the possibility of his conducting a formal interview.

Despite his mounting eagerness, Anne sensed he hadn't been thoroughly convinced by her performance, and they had played a game of cat and mouse.

"I hope you won't be insulted, Ms. Billings, if I'm not completely convinced that you're ready to sign on to this."

"And you shouldn't be convinced," Anne had said, not wanting to give in too quickly. Her goal was to stall him. "I haven't made up my mind yet. I need a little more time."

They were walking along Third Avenue as traffic thickened and horns tooted, and snow flurries drifted down.

He'd given her a side glance. "I hope you won't try to run away. If you do, I will find you. I want you to sign onto this voluntarily but, if you don't, then I'm willing to take whatever steps I must. The truth is, Ms. Billings, exceptional opportunities like you don't come around more than once in a lifetime, if that."

His words brought a little shiver rippling up her spine, but she'd kept up her calm act, speaking casually. "And where would I go? I don't have any family or friends, other than Constance and Leon, and I don't have any identification."

He shoved his hands into his pockets. "I'd be willing to bet that you're smart and resourceful. You have a will, and I'm sure you could find a way."

"You overestimate me. I'm lonely, confused and, quite frankly, very weary. It's becoming clear to me that I'm going to have to start a brand-new life in this time... in this world."

Anne saw that Alex liked the sound of that.

They had stopped at Alex's black SUV. "Once the interview is approved, and we move on to the next phase of the investigation, I'll be able to help you with that. We'll find you the perfect place where you can start fresh, with all the resources you'll need for a happy life."

Anne had forced her lips into a pleasant smile. "How lovely that sounds."

But Anne had no intention whatsoever of living anywhere except in England. There, she would search the past and try to learn what had happened to her parents and Tommy.

"Are you going back to Leon's apartment?" Alex asked.

"No, I don't think so. I'd like to walk and think. It will do me good."

"Can I give you a ride anywhere?"

"No, thank you."

He gazed directly into her eyes, boring into her, searching for truth. "You say you need more time to think about it. How much time do you need?"

"Two days. I have the phone number you gave me. I'll call you in two days with my answer."

That's where they'd left it.

AFTER STUDYING HER MAP of Central Park, Anne left the taxi on Fifth Avenue at East 79th Street and entered Central Park, walking past the *Group of Bears* statue and a playground. She continued on the footpath which skirted the south side of the museum, going through the stone Greywacke Arch and turning right. When the Obelisk came into view, she slowed her pace, feeling a rising sense of foreboding. She approached it cautiously.

Anne stopped, turned the collar of her coat up against the busy wind and moved ahead. She'd done her homework and knew that the Obelisk, also known as "Cleopatra's Needle," was the oldest man-made object in Central Park and the oldest outdoor monument in New York City. It was more than three-thousand years old and stood sixty-nine feet high.

The Obelisk was part of a pair. The second was in London, on the bank of the Thames River, close to the Embankment underground station. Two large bronze sphinxes lay on either side of the Needle.

She had read that the two Obelisks had been commissioned about 1450 BCE to commemorate Pharaoh Thutmose III's thirtieth year of reign. Each Obelisk had been carved from a single slab of quarried rose granite. Egypt had gifted the London Obelisk in 1871, and the Obelisk to New York in 1881.

The monument was surrounded by magnolia and crabapple trees, which Anne thought would be lovely in the spring. The paved terrace had benches arranged in a circle around the Obelisk, and because her feet hurt, she sat on one of the benches, feeling the cold seep into her bones as she replayed the conversation she'd just had with Alex Fogel.

She had to escape New York, and soon. She couldn't let him trap her, and trap her, he would. There was steel purpose in his eyes, and she'd sensed a gnawing determination in the man that terrified her.

The thought of being trapped turned her stomach to acid, as if she'd taken poison.

Despite the cold, Anne sat with her agitated emotions and cast her eyes about the area. She'd been flung into 2008 somewhere near here. With desperate hope and out of urgent necessity, Anne's mind turned to considering improbable things, wild things. Perhaps there *was* a time doorway or secret passage near the Obelisk that would send her back to 1944... send her back to Tommy and her parents. Events she would have once thought impossible now were reality, so why couldn't there be a time tunnel or portal that could shoot her back to where she'd come from?

Anne breathed shallowly, willing it to be so; willing some extraordinary crack in time to appear suddenly before her, like a shaft of lightning, so she could dart into the light and fly back to 1944.

On her feet, she circled the Obelisk, her every nerve on alert. She circled it three times, but nothing happened. Undeterred, she left the terrace for the grass and began to pace, searching for a sign, for anything that might feel unusual; for anything that might seem out of place; for any radiant, pulsing light.

When a couple looked on curiously, she didn't notice them. At first, she walked at right angles to the Obelisk; then diagonally, taking brisk strides, her every sense awake, her eyes probing. When three children ran by, she ignored them. When tourists paused to study her, thinking she was involved in some odd ritual, she looked away from them, oblivious, a touch of panic growing in her eyes.

A mounting desperation nudged her on until the wind burned her cheeks and she grew tired, and the folly and futility of her quest became sadly obvious. In defeat, she trudged back to one of the benches and sat. Waves of despair cruised over her, heating her one minute and chilling her the next.

She reached into her purse for the cell phone Constance had given her, a RIM Blackberry Curve. Anne had only used it twice, both times to call Constance. She stared at the thing, a wonder and a miracle, like the computers of this time, like nearly everything of this time. Why was she feeling repulsion for all these modern do-dads, so her father would have probably called them? There was too much information crashing in at the touch of a button or the click of a mouse. There was too much noise and talking static.

Anne was about to call Constance and bring her up-to-date when she stopped, struggling with the phone to find Leon's number. She thought he should know that his uncle was on to him.

She touched the speed dial and waited as the phone rang twice. Leon's voice was loud. "Anne? Is everything okay?"

Anne shut her eyes, turning away from two heavy men who were studying the Obelisk. "Your uncle is on to us."

"What?"

She explained everything, finishing with, "After I left him, I took a taxi to the Obelisk in Central Park. That's where I am."

Leon's voice was high and strained. "Oh, man… that's so messed up. I mean, no way. I mean, you shouldn't have left the apartment. No way you should have left. Did you wear the blonde wig?"

Anne's voice held frustration. "Yes, Leon, for all the good it did. He knew I was staying with you."

"Oh, wow… I didn't know…"

"Leon, I have only two days, and maybe not even that, before he wants me to be, as he put it, interviewed, which actually means locked up in some secret place and put under a bloody microscope, so to speak. Interrogated like I'm some criminal. I'll never get out and back to England."

"I've got to think," Leon said. "Did you call Constance?"

"No. Constance can't get me a passport, Leon, and I don't want to alarm her. I don't mean to sound ungrateful, but can you please call your friend and tell him it's imperative that I get that passport now? I don't trust your uncle, Leon. I know he'll be watching your place and he could come storming in at any time and take me off to God knows where."

Leon sputtered. "Okay, okay. I'll call my guy. I'll call and tell him we've got to have your passport, like now."

"I'm not going back to your place, Leon."

"What?"

"I'll find somewhere else to stay."

"But where?"

"I don't know where, but someplace where your uncle can't find me. I'll figure it out. When you get the passport, call me. I'm cold to my bones, Leon. I'm hanging up and finding someplace to warm myself. Please, hurry with the passport."

CHAPTER 25

A nne sat on the edge of the hotel bed in darkness, listening to the sounds of the city below; the murmur of traffic; the car horns; a siren passing; the unnerving, chopping blades of a helicopter. They sounded like violence and made her think of the war.

She struggled to control her emotions, fighting tears one moment and letting them come the next. Finally, she mastered them, vowing to stop crying and come up with solutions.

Once she'd arrived in her room, she'd pulled off the wig and tossed it into the wastebasket. Next, she'd made the dreaded call to Constance, explaining what had happened. Predictably, she'd gone into a rage, cursing Leon, cursing Alex Fogel, and cursing herself for letting Anne go.

"Where are you, Anne?" she demanded.

"I don't know, some hotel in the West 60s. I was so cold and scared. I just walked in, booked a room and paid with the credit card you gave me. I'm sorry I keep spending your money."

"I don't give a damn about the money, Anne, I care about you. Get in a cab and come back here."

"Constance... I can't. I don't want that man knowing where I am."

"Don't worry about him. I'll call Senator Arlen Paxton and put a stop to this right now."

"That won't stop him," Anne said. "I saw it in his eyes."

"Well, I have a handgun and, so help me God, I'll use it on him if he tries to break into my place. Now come back to me, Anne. It sickens me to think you're alone in some sleazy hotel. I want you where I can protect you."

Anne stood in the center of the snug room, one thought tripping over another. "I just don't know, Constance. I don't want you involved with this anymore. I truly believe Leon's uncle is dangerous."

"Believe me, Anne, if he gets in my way, I'll take care of him. Now, get out of there and jump into a cab."

Anne felt resistance. "I don't know. I think I want to spend the night here, alone. I need time to think."

Constance sighed into the phone. "Anne... listen to me. Once we get that passport, we are off to the airport. You'll never see that man again."

"He will follow us."

"I don't give a damn if he does. Anyway, I have an idea about that. I'll share it with you when you get here."

Anne moved toward the two windows, pulled the cord and parted the heavy beige curtains that looked out of her tenth-floor window. There were shadowy buildings nearby and, in the distance, the shiny lights of New York.

"I'll stay the night, Constance. Just one night. As I said, I need to be alone. Please understand."

"I think you're being foolish," Constance said with irritation. "But if that's what you want, then so be it. In the morning, get here as soon as you can. I have a feeling we're going to have to work fast."

After hanging up, Anne remained still. The darkness seemed alive, with roaming ghosts from her past. Was that her father in the corner? Was that wheezing sound her mother breathing? Was Tommy hiding behind the curtains, playing peek-a-boo, snickering at her?

On impulse, she snatched up her purse and left the room, pausing in the brightly lit hallway to finger-comb her hair and ensure she had the smart card to open her door.

She was the only person in the elevator, and the overhead light seemed to pour down on her like a noonday sun. At the lobby, she left the elevator, took a bracing breath and glanced about cautiously, not seeing anyone suspicious.

The hotel lounge was a cozy room, with a long mahogany bar and a row of red leather, padded barstools, illuminated by hanging, amber lamps. Several round tables were occupied, and the music emanating from overhead speakers was soft rock.

Anne had never sat at a bar alone. In pubs back home, she'd either stood with friends or taken her pint to a table. She had no idea what the protocol was. Was it proper to sit on one of those stools? All the tables were taken, and she spotted a woman alone, perched on a barstool, scrolling through her cell phone.

Two middle-aged men in suits were lost in conversation and, at the far end, a young man in stylish clothes was bent over a mug of beer, his troubled expression suggesting a bad day at the office.

Anne took a chance and sat on the stool closest to the lobby. She relaxed a little when no one seemed to notice or care.

When the thin, attractive bartender stepped over, she was taken by his thick dark hair, pushed up and spiked. It was an odd hairstyle, she thought, but appealing. She quickly took in his fine, handsome face, his friendly eyes, and the black shirt and dark pants that made him a bit fetching. He was a momentary, pleasant distraction, and Anne was grateful for it.

"Hey there," he said, lightly. "What can I get you?"

She met his eyes and smiled. "I guess I'll have a pint of something."

"A pint?"

"Or whatever you have."

"How about a cold mug of pale ale, or an IPA?"

Anne raised her shoulders. "I don't know. The pale ale sounds lovely, thank you."

"You have a great Italian accent, there," the bartender said, with a playful wink.

"Italian?" Anne exclaimed with an arched eyebrow.

"Just a stupid joke. Are you from London?"

Why did the question sound strange to her? "London... Yes, well actually, I'm from Stratford, a district in the East End of London. Do you know London?"

"No, not really. I was there once on a high school trip, but I don't remember much except Big Ben and the Tower of London."

Anne felt a sudden nostalgia for her country, and she turned reflective. "It's a lovely place, with nice people and good pubs."

"I went to a pub or two, but I was underage. An older buddy of mine ordered me a pint, and it nearly knocked me on my ass. I guess I was used to Budweiser."

Anne smiled. "Yes, the ales can make you a bit wobbly if you're not used to it."

"And that pint was pricey, because he made me pay for it."

"Really? When I left, a pint cost about one shilling and sixpence."

The bartender cocked his head as if he didn't hear correctly. "Shilling?"

"Yes, but that was..." she stopped, suddenly remembering where she was and what year she was living in.

"But the shilling isn't used anymore, is it?" the bartender asked.

Anne forced a nervous smile. She had no idea what the currency was, and she had the irrational, fear-driven thought that he'd find her out and call the police. "Well... of course things have changed. Things always change, don't they?"

The bartender searched her face for signs of a joke. He didn't see it and stepped back. "I'll just get that draft for you."

The bartender soon returned with a cold mug, the head foaming. "Here you go. Sorry, but it costs a little more than a shilling, not that I know how much a shilling is worth."

Avoiding his eyes, she handed him her credit card. "I'll just have the one."

After Anne signed the credit card slip, the bartender remained, a curious glint in his eyes. "Are you traveling on business?"

"No," she said quickly. Then softer, she said, "I mean, no."

"Are your folks over there, in England?"

Anne took a sip of the beer. It tasted good, so she drank more, needing to ease her rattled nerves.

"Yes…"

"I'm from Denver," the bartender said.

To hide her ignorance of not knowing where Denver was, Anne took another generous drink. "Do you miss it?"

"Yeah, I guess. Sometimes you miss your real home, don't you?"

Anne nodded, feeling the truth of his words flow through her until a pang of sadness lowered her eyes.

The bartender said, "My mother could cook. I mean, she could really cook… anything. I used to eat her cooking and think, this is good, but I was too stupid to know that I'd probably never get food that good again, not for the rest of my life."

Anne looked up. "You should go home and see her. I'm sure she'd love to cook for you."

His smile was brief. "She passed on… two years ago."

"I'm so sorry. You're young to have lost your mum."

"As they say, you only have one, and ain't that the truth?"

Anne smiled, her thoughts drifting back, the slight buzz from the beer making her nostalgic. "Yes... and it's always the little things you remember, isn't it? Like my mother's minced tarts at Christmas. And I was just thinking about her pickled eggs yesterday. We'd share them with bread and tea, and we'd dig our spoons into a lovely jar of strawberry jam."

Anne drifted into a pleasant recollection, the beer beginning to loosen the tension and release the rigid control of her mind. It felt good to talk about her past to a stranger, a man she'd never see again. What did it matter if she sounded a little crazy? Wasn't she entitled to be a little crazy, after all she'd been through? So Anne continued to talk and feel the pleasure of it.

"Mum and I would take a market basket and go shopping for things... Oh, so many things there were before the war, even though times were hard for many people. But that was before rationing."

"What war was that?" the bartender asked, growing suspicious.

Anne ignored him. For the moment, she didn't care where she was or what year it was. Her loneliness and homesickness took center stage.

"And sometimes Mum's sister, Clementine, would accompany us. She lived in Kensington Park. She was killed in 1940. Mum cried for days. I suppose I did, as well. It seems so many years ago and yet, it seems like yesterday."

The bartender kept his wary eyes on her. Although the pretty woman looked perfectly normal, he now suspected she was mentally unbalanced.

Anne drank distractedly, nearly draining the mug. She chatted on. "During the Blitz, a fifty-pound German bomb fell directly onto a trench shelter where Aunt Clementine and others had gathered. That in October 1940. Rescuers managed to find only forty-eight identifiable bodies. One hundred and four souls perished. It was such a wretched day for us. Mum never really recovered from that."

The bartender had had enough. "Will there be anything else?" he asked, suddenly indifferent, the friendliness gone from his eyes.

Anne looked at him, sorry she'd lost a momentary friend. "No... I'll be going."

Upstairs in her dark room, Anne lay back into the pillows, her thoughts rambling and unfocused. She fumbled for ideas, for solutions, for ways she could return to 1944. "I have to find Tommy," she said aloud. And to the darkness, and to those ghosts who were hiding in the darkness, she said, "You can understand that, can't you?"

CHAPTER 26

The next morning, Anne sat at the hotel restaurant counter eating a hardy breakfast of fried eggs, bacon, toast, and coffee. She was forcing herself to eat, knowing she'd need all her strength in the days to come.

Two well-dressed men, speaking in low, agitated voices, sat nearby. One was heavy, the other thin. The heavy one said he had private information from a man at an investment company. "So that broker says I should buy back into the market now. 'Buy low,' he says. I told him he was crazy. I told him, 'Where's the bottom? Right now, the market's a falling knife and everybody knows you don't try to catch a falling knife.' Dammit! The Dow lost six-hundred and eighty points yesterday. The paper said it's the twelfth worst percentage one-day decline ever. We're not getting the truth about what the hell's really going on. It's all bullshit."

The thin man said, "Where do you get any truth when everybody's in a panic out there? Hell, the damn sky is falling, and what's the Fed doing? Nothing. We're in for a bad recession, and there's no doubt about it."

The heavy man said, "Well, I'm screwed bigtime. I've already lost over four-hundred thousand dollars. And that was just last week."

The thin man pursed his lips and whistled. "Get out while you can. Sell it all and get out. We haven't hit bottom yet. Cash is king right now."

The men sat hunched over cups of coffee, their expressions grim. Anne could smell their anxiety and, already having enough of her own, she turned away from them and glanced at the clock on the wall, right above the tidy row of mini cereal boxes.

It was almost ten o'clock and Leon was late. On the phone over an hour ago, he'd said he'd meet her at 9:30 in the restaurant.

Anne sipped her coffee and tried not to think, which was impossible. Had his uncle snatched him away? And if he had, would Leon talk? If Alex had grabbed his nephew, would he find the passport Leon was bringing to her?

On the phone, Leon's voice had been bursting with the stellar news. "Anne, I have it! Your passport!"

When she told him where she was, he said he'd be there at 9:30 sharp.

Anne twisted around, glancing toward the restaurant entrance. Where was he? She felt perspiration pop out on her forehead and upper lip.

Anne had called Constance with the good news, and she'd shouted out a loud, "Yes!" Then she'd said, "Alright, listen up. I have a plan, just in case that CIA jerk comes after us. Don't come here, Anne. Stay where you are. Give me the name of the hotel and I'll come to you. Do you have a bag packed?"

"No... I have nothing. I didn't go back to Leon's apartment after I saw his uncle."

"Doesn't matter. I'll bring some necessaries and clothes you didn't take to Leon's. Anything else you need, we'll buy online in England. I'll book the flight now and be over in about three hours. Don't leave. Now tell me where you are and your room number."

Anne drained the last of her coffee at five minutes after ten. There was still no sign of Leon, and Anne felt the raw, mean panic of a wild animal. His uncle had surely caught him. She and Leon should have known better, and come up with another, safer plan.

She glanced over her shoulder yet again, her eyes fierce. That's when she saw him. A teenage boy entered the restaurant, gangly and shuffling, shouldering a backpack, wearing a black ski cap and a frayed army jacket. He paused at the hostess stand while his eyes searched for, and then found, Anne. They narrowed on her in recognition.

Anne drew herself upright.

When the hostess approached, the kid pointed at Anne and then started toward her, sliding the backpack off his shoulder as he approached.

He drew up, then slouched. "Are you Anne B?"

She looked him over, his narrow hips and long, straight legs. He had an angelic face, with smooth, pink cheeks and dark, shy eyes.

"Yes..."

He reached into his backpack and drew out a manilla envelope and handed it to her. "This is for you. The guy who gave it to me told me what you looked like and where you'd be."

Anne looked at the envelope, her heart kicking. She took it. "Where... Where was he when he gave you this?"

"On the corner of Third and 112th Street. He told me to tell you he couldn't make it."

"Did he say why?"

"No."

"What time did he give you the envelope?"

The kid shrugged. "I don't know... Maybe a half hour ago. I rode down on my bike."

"Was there anyone with him when he handed you the envelope?"

"No, just him, but he kept... like, you know, looking around. He was stressed."

"Did he pay you? I don't have any money."

"No problem. He took care of it. I've got to go. I'm already late for school."

Before Anne could thank him, he swung around and started off, hunching into his backpack.

UPSTAIRS, ANNE CHAIN-LOCKED THE DOOR, sat down on the edge of the bed, pinched the two brass pins together and opened the flap. With a quick intake of breath, she snaked her hand inside and drew out the passport.

She peered inside and saw something else—a note—and reached for it. It was folded once, a perfect fold with a perfect crease. She opened it and began to read. The script was clear, if small.

Ms. Billings: don't get angry, but you'll notice I changed your name from Anne Billings to Anne Watson. My friend said it would be best, especially because my uncle knows your name now and will search for you as Billings.

I'm writing this fast. My uncle's on his way, so I have to be quick. Good luck. I hope you make it back home... all the way. Don't worry, I won't tell Uncle Alex anything... just enough. What's he gonna do, torture me? It was cool meeting you.

Leon

Anne paced her room, lay on the bed, flopping left and then right, battling charging nerves. Finally, she swung off the bed and paced on until 11:30. When she heard a light knock, she jerked. Hardly breathing, she crept to the door.

She whispered. "Who is it?"

"Constance. Let me in."

Anne turned the lock, released the chain, and swung the door open. Constance slipped inside, glancing up and down the hallway.

Once the locks were secured, Constance opened her arms and Anne stepped into her embrace, relieved to be with her friend and protector. She held back tears, but her heart was full of emotion.

Constance stroked her hair. "Go ahead, Anne, cry if you need to. You deserve a good cry. I'd cry too, if I had any tears left, but I cried them all out when Ashley died."

"I've cried enough," Anne said. "I'm ready to move on now."

They held the embrace for a time, and then Anne drew back and handed Constance Leon's note. After reading it, she grimaced.

"Yes, he changed my last name."

"Damn," Constance exclaimed. "I'll have to change your airplane ticket. All right, I'll do this now, and then let's get out of here. I've got a limo waiting outside to take us to the airport."

Constance pulled her cell phone and dialed, glancing over at Anne. "We can't trust Leon, Anne. I wouldn't put it past Alex Fogel to beat the truth out of his nephew. I had a government friend look Mr. Fogel up. He's worked in Russia, the Mideast and the Far East. He's fiercely competitive and highly intelligent, and he's considered one of the best interrogators in the agency."

Fear, sour and hot, churned in Anne's stomach.

Constance held the phone to her ear and shot Anne a bitter stare. "I have a friend in London who will lend me a gun. I'll shoot that CIA bastard if I have to."

PART 2

CHAPTER 27
London 1944

"SO WHAT WAS LONDON like before the war started?" First Lieutenant Kenneth Cassidy Taylor asked.

Anne Billings' dancing eyes flitted up at him. He was a tall man, well over six feet, with an athletic build and a natural grace. "Do you want all the bits and bobs, including the underside?"

"Yes, especially the underside," he answered with a wink. "I think the underside is the best side. On second thought, you can keep the bits and bobs."

"You Americans are quite cheeky, I think."

"Cheeky? What exactly does that mean? I've heard it used, but I was too proud to ask the British guys what it means."

"In your case, it means... well, let me see now... I'd say, a bit amusing, with a dash of impertinence."

"Impertinence? Such a classy word for such a Midwestern guy from Chicago."

Anne laughed merrily, enjoying their afternoon walk in Hyde Park. It was the perfect rambling day, with sparkling sun and a soft autumn breeze that caressed the skin.

"Let's just say, Lieutenant Taylor, that you wear cheeky very well."

He linked his arm in hers and smiled into her eyes. "I'll take that as a compliment and leave it at that. I can see I'm treading on thin ice."

Ken felt the power of Anne's attractiveness, enjoying her killer smile and the tender bloom on her cheeks. "I'm so glad you could get away."

"And I'm thrilled to bits that you got your leave."

Ken's eyes clouded over. "I deserve it. The last two missions were rough. There was a lot of flak and fighters, and we lost a lot of planes and good men."

Anne felt the stomach-pit dread of his words. "How many missions do you have left to fly?"

"Ten... That is, if they don't add five more onto it."

"I hate this war so much," Anne said.

Ken resettled his shoulders as Anne watched two squirrels chase about, and then dart off for a nearby tree.

"But let's forget about the war now," Ken said, forcing a bright smile. "We have blue skies over London, which is a minor miracle; we have a cool wind and, so far, there haven't been any air raid sirens. Maybe the Germans are taking a day off, too."

"I doubt that. They never rest," Anne said, aridly. "Not one day do they rest. Sometimes I think I should take Tommy and leave London, just run away from the air raids, the barrage balloons, and those gun emplacements over there, where flower gardens used to be."

Ken followed her eyes. "Yeah, it must be hard to see anti-aircraft guns and rocket launchers in your parks. There must be more than sixty over there."

"Don't get me wrong, I'm glad we have them when the Nazis are bombing... it's just that we're always surrounded by war in London, and it's gone on for so long. Sometimes I think it will never end."

"You *could* leave London, couldn't you, now that you left your job at Bletchley Park?"

"Yes, I could. I have an aunt in Devonshire. She's always writing and asking Mum, Tommy and me to come. But then Dad would be alone, wouldn't he? Mum wouldn't leave him. But, anyway, London's my home and I don't want to run off like a scared bunny rabbit when things are so bad."

They took a winding path and strolled past park benches, tall hedges and an elderly couple dressed in faded, old clothes. Ken tipped his hat to them and they smiled. The man said, "Best of luck to ya, Yank."

"Thank you, sir," Ken said. When they had moved away, Ken glanced back. "I see a lot of people wearing old clothes. The States should be sending more over here."

"Better to have your bombers and soldiers. We'll get by with rationing and old clothes."

"You Brits are a tough bunch," Ken said. "I admire that."

"We have to be, don't we? We're not going to let the Germans invade us, thank you very much. Never."

Bicyclers wheeled by, soldiers roamed with their girls, and two matronly women attended a vegetable garden, hoeing and turning the earth. Anne explained that the gardens were part of Britain's 'Dig for Victory' campaign, created to counter dwindling food imports from overseas. They were also an important boost for morale.

Ken wanted to steer the subject away from the war. "How is Tommy?"

"He's well, thank you. He wants to be a pilot, like his Dad was... like a lot of little boys. He says he wants to fly a Spitfire, but he calls it a Spitsflyer."

Ken laughed. "I like that. Very descriptive."

"My Mum wants to evacuate him to a school in Addlestone, but I don't want to."

"Is the school far?"

"No, just outside London, but I want him with me. I don't want him with strangers at a time like this. He needs his Mum, don't you think?"

"Of course he does."

"And he's good company for my Mum. She's so worried about the bombs, and so am I, but I can't part with him. Not anymore. He's my own little boy."

"I'd love to meet him."

"I'll bring him one day. Oh, but I did bring some snaps of him."

"Snaps?"

"Photographs."

They sat on a bench and Anne removed the black-and-white photos from her purse. She held them up for Ken to see. "Here he's a little pouty face, and here he's all happy smiles."

Ken studied them. "He's a handsome boy. He looks like a little Alan Ladd."

"You'd like him, Kenneth. He's as bright as the sun and not as frightened of the bombs as he once was. There was a time, awhile back, when the bombing was so bad, he wouldn't talk. That happens to a lot of kids. But now that I'm not working anymore and can be with him, he's much better."

Anne replaced the photos and then turned to face Ken, her eyes downcast. "Am I being selfish keeping him in London instead of moving to Devonshire, and away from the war?"

Ken took her hand and looked deeply into her eyes. "You know what's right, Anne. In your heart, you know."

"Thanks for that. It was so awful at the start of the war. Everyone was conflicted. When children were evacuated to safer regions, parents were terrified that they'd never see them again. And many parents whose children had been evacuated in September 1939 decided to bring them home again. By January 1940, almost half of the children had returned home. Children should be with their parents, especially when there's so much death and destruction. We have to get through this together, as a country and a family."

Ken nodded. "As I said, I admire this country. When I look around at the bombed-out buildings and all the destruction, I'm amazed how you people can keep going. I wish folks back home could see you. It would be an inspiration to them."

Anne presented her face into the sun, closing her eyes. "Oh, this is lovely, isn't it? Such a perfect day it is. When I close my eyes like this, I imagine that the war is over and it's spring, and all the guns are gone, and all the flowers are in bloom. It will happen. One day, this war will be over, and we'll really live life again."

Lieutenant Taylor looked at her, feeling the rise of warm pleasure, feeling all the stress he carried in his soul relax and melt away.

He caressed her hand, his eyes exploring her face. "You're so pretty, Anne, and so smart, and so easy to be with. My folks would fall in love with you."

Anne's eyes shifted and found his. She smiled, tenderly. "What a nice thing to say. It gives me hope… It makes me wonder about Chicago."

"You'd like it there."

She looked away, her expression suddenly gloomy. "It's so far away."

"Not so far."

She smiled at him. "Well, it's fun to play pretend, isn't it?"

His eyes narrowed on her. "I don't want to pretend, Anne."

Anne felt hopelessness and anxiety, but she smiled them away. "This morning, I was remembering how we parted at the underground in Piccadilly, the night we met at the dance at the Rainbow Corner all those weeks ago. Who could ever forget that name? It was anything but a rainbow."

"You changed the subject, Anne."

"Because I have to. Things are too uncertain; too, I don't know, unreachable, at least for now."

Ken readjusted himself on the bench. "Yeah, I suppose so."

"But you do remember that night, don't you?"

He grinned with pleasure. "Yeah, you know I do. I'll never forget the wall-to-wall people. And who could dance? Everybody was bumping into everybody else. Now that I think of it, I don't even remember how I got there."

"But we managed to dance, didn't we? I'm so glad you asked me."

"You were the prettiest girl in the place and, when you smiled at me, well, I was a goner. It was kind of like magic that drew me to you... that still draws me to you."

Anne's eyes traveled over his lean face, taking in his fine features and dignified air. "What are your parents like?"

"They're good people. Dad's an attorney, or, as you say over here, a barrister, and Mom's a housewife."

"And you said you have a brother?"

"Yes, Gary. He's in the Navy, fighting in the Pacific."

"What's Chicago like?"

"It's a big, muscular, bustling town, filled with hardworking people. There are a lot of swell neighborhood spots to eat, where you can have a beer and get together with friends. It's cold as the dickens in the winter when the wind blows off Lake Michigan and, in the summer, you hang out on the Lake and go to the ball parks to watch baseball. It's a great town to raise a family."

Anne considered that as she watched a yellow butterfly flit about a hydrangea and then flutter away.

Ken kissed her hand and then leaned over, pushed up the bill of his cap and kissed her warm, moist lips.

When they broke the kiss, Ken held her eyes, exploring their depths. "I miss you, Anne."

"But I'm here."

"But not when I'm flying at twenty-five thousand feet."

She gave a quick shake of her head. "I'm not sure I want to be way up there at twenty-five thousand feet, Lieutenant Taylor."

"Well, it is cold."

"And very high."

"And I think of you, and I think to myself, is she thinking of me?"

"You know I am. You know I want this terrible war to be over, so you don't have to fly your bomber over Germany."

Ken's forehead pinched in thought.

"What are you thinking, Kenneth?"

"I love the way you say Kenneth. It's breathy and intimate, and very romantic."

Her smile was a flash of easy desire. "And so I love your name, and your blue/gray eyes... and right now I hear the motors in your head grinding away."

Ken nodded, his mood changing. "I was just wondering what it was like for you before the war... I mean, how was it with your husband? I guess I think about that sometimes when I'm flying. Were you in love?"

Anne lowered her chin and sighed. "Yes, Kenneth. We were in love, at least for a time, anyway. I was so young. It seems so long ago, and yet it seems a week ago. As Dad would say, time is both long and short and nobody can grab the thing by the tail and pin it down."

Ken grinned. "I like that."

Anne continued, going inside herself, to a small, sad place. "What I remember so keenly and dream about so often is what it was like when all the lights in London went out for the first time in 1939. We knew then that the war was about to begin. Basil and I had been planning to be married in two months, but that night, the night the lights went out, we decided not to wait. We decided to get married straight away."

Anne stared into the middle distance as if she were seeing the past projected onto a movie screen. "We were standing on the footway of Hungerford Bridge, midway across the Thames. London was lit up like a dreamland, in a brilliance that dazzled the sky, and then one by one, different areas of the city went dark, as if someone were pulling a switch."

Anne paused, inhaling a breath and letting it out. "The city reminded me of a patchwork quilt of lights, and they were being extinguished, first one and then another, until there was only one patch still lit. I held my breath, and my hands formed fists. I vividly remember doing this, because I squeezed my hands so tightly that my fingernails dug into my palms. And then the last lights went out. My heart sank, and we both shut our eyes. There was nothing more to see, anyway. We knew then that war was inevitable, and that Basil would have to fight. I had never anticipated that we would have to fight a war in the dark, or that the smallest light could bring down German bombs."

Kenneth let her words sink in. "It must have been terrifying."

Anne looked at him. "When the Gaiety Theater closed, its brown velvet curtains drew a high price at auction. They were converted into excellent blackout curtains."

Anne sat up, forcing a smile. "But no more war talk or sad talk. We're together for a whole day and most of the night. What do you have planned for us tonight?"

Ken grew excited. "All right now, close your eyes and imagine it."

Anne laughed, but did so. "I'm ready."

"Squeeze your eyes shut."

"Come on, Kenneth, tell me."

"Okay, here goes. What is the most swell place in town to get a juicy steak?"

"Well, let me think."

"No thinking. We're going to The Ritz."

Anne's eyes popped open in surprise. "The Ritz?"

"So go put on your best dress and your dancing shoes, and pray there's no air raid tonight."

On impulse, Anne reached up, wrapped a hand around Ken's neck and pulled him down for a kiss. When they broke it, Ken lifted an eyebrow. "Holy smoke. Now why didn't I take you to The Ritz on our first date instead of to the Coventry Street Lyons?"

"Because we got caught in an air raid and had to spend the night. But the breakfast was lovely. I remember everything you ordered. Now let me see," she said, grinning and glancing up into the blue sky to gather her thoughts. She ticked off the items on one hand. "Porridge, bacon, fried bread and marmalade."

"And a pot of tea because you don't like coffee," Ken added.

"Yes, and the tea was perfection. All right, I have to rush home and check on Mum and Tommy." She rose. "What time shall we meet at the Ritz?"

Lieutenant Taylor pushed to his feet. "Seven o'clock. That will give me time to get back to the Savoy and clean up."

He bent and kissed her, a long passionate kiss.

When their lips parted, Ken said, "Anne... You know I've fallen in love with you, don't you?"

She touched his lower lip with a finger. "Yes, Kenneth. I know... And I'm so scared for both of us."

CHAPTER 28
London 1944

First Lieutenant Kenneth Taylor wandered in a kind of fog, despite the bright, sunny day. He was troubled and worried. He'd left Anne an hour before and she'd never said she loved him. He'd seen the conflict building in her eyes while he talked, and he'd hoped she'd say the words he was waiting to hear, but she hadn't. Instead, she'd touched his lips and his cheek with her delicate hand and said she'd see him at seven by the velvet circular couch in The Ritz Hotel lobby.

So Ken Taylor had walked Anne to the underground, kissed her gently and then watched her go. He'd shoved his hands into his pockets and started on a brisk walk, cursing the war and his bad timing.

What a time to fall in love, he thought. He needed to walk the streets and think. But London in 1944 wasn't an atmosphere conducive to clear, clean thought.

Prostitutes wandered the streets of Mayfair in their gaudy finery. Soldiers rambled over with shy smiles, or hard stares, or confident nods. The girls charged between ten shillings and £1 an encounter, and since shop girls could earn as little as £1 a week, it was an easy temptation. At night, the girls would stand in doorways and flash pencil torches on their faces.

Coming from Chicago, Lieutenant Taylor wasn't naïve, but he had principles and pride, and he thought all the loose living and careless attitudes were further proof that the world had gone insane. It was all about living for the day because tomorrow you might be dead.

"Get as much out of life as you can today, Lieutenant, because tomorrow you may be dead for all eternity," his bombardier, Joe Paxton, had said while they sat on the train heading for London. "Hey, we've ten more missions to go and that might as well be fifty. You know we're going to be flying to Berlin, where the flak is so thick you can walk on it, and if we don't get air support from the P-51s, the German 109s will cut us to pieces. More head-on attacks, and more dead pilots and crews."

Ken idled along the streets, battling his thoughts and depression. It was one thing to focus on flying, keeping his B-17 in tight formation, concentrating on the job you had to do, and it was another thing to push thoughts of Anne from his mind. He'd fallen for her. He'd fallen hard and there was no going back. He didn't want to let her go. He wanted to marry her and take her home to Chicago. Was he being a sap, especially if she didn't love him?

LATER, AFTER KEN HAD A NAP, a shower and a fresh shave, he left the Savoy—anxious to meet Anne at The Ritz. London was packed with men in various kinds of uniforms, wearing khaki, navy blue, steel blue and forest green. The pubs were crowded and loud, and Ken heard snatches of lusty songs bursting out from men who were well along on their night of drinking.

The nightly blackout was strictly enforced, up and down the streets, by wardens, but Ken often saw the flare of a cigarette lighter. He also saw a line of soldiers walking arm in arm, maybe ten or more, heading for some bistro or pub. As he passed two such pubs, the singing and shouting were deafening, but no one seemed to care. Despite all the ugliness of war, there was friendship and laughter and song and, if it was possible to find a good part of war, Ken thought this was it.

KEN WAS WAITING INSIDE The Ritz's lobby when Anne entered, saw him and went over, expectation hanging in the air. After a kiss, Ken stepped back, checking her out.

"Nice coat."

"Thank you, Lieutenant Taylor. It's part of the 'make do and mend' fashion."

Anne released the buttons and held it open, revealing her printed, rayon crepe dress, artfully modeling it for him, turning this way and that.

Overwhelmed, he pressed a hand into his cheek, taking her in, her full red lips, her victory curls and her glowing eyes. "Holy mackerel, you look like a million bucks."

Anne lifted her chin, proudly. "A pretty dress, a new perm, a new me. Well, the dress isn't new; I bought it at Swan & Edgar in 1940, I think."

Ken offered her his arm and they swept off to the below-stairs Grill Room, which was called 'La Popote'. The walls were packed with sandbags, kept in place by wooden props and naked metal struts. Graffiti adorned the woodwork, and candles burned in the necks of wine bottles set on utility tablecloths. A kind of makeshift candelabra, composed of even more bottles, lit the modest dance floor, crowded with swaying dancers.

Displayed on the wall near the dancefloor was a poster depicting a Union Jack, with Winston Churchill's bulldog face in the background, and a haggard soldier in the foreground holding the hand of a frightened mother clutching her child. The bold black caption read:

PEOPLE OF BRITAIN!
KEEP BUGGERING ON!

Anne's and Ken's table was somewhat private, placed in the back corner in dim light. On the stage, the swing band was romping through the song *Shoo, Shoo Baby*, and the mood was loose and festive, the cigarette smoke hovering in stringy clouds.

They danced before their steaks arrived and danced after they'd finished eating. Back on the dance floor, they were pushed and shoved by the dancing crush. The music was bouncy, the smiles broad, the booze plentiful.

When Anne stopped to draw a breath, a loose-limbed sailor cut in.

"Hey, beautiful, can I have this dance?"

"Not on your life, sailor," Ken shot back. "She's all mine."

Unsteady on his feet, the sailor's glassy-eyed stare fell on Ken. He shrugged. "Okay, then how about you and me go for a little dance, fly boy?"

Ken playfully shoved him back into the crowd, both men laughing.

Ken shouted to Anne, "I bet the MPs will drag his hung-over body out of jail in the morning."

"It's getting stuffy in here," Anne said. "Want to go somewhere else?"

Outside, Anne and Ken strolled through a city in darkness, with its cries of laughter, honking horns and the dreaded anticipation of an air raid.

"Where would you like to go?" Ken asked.

"I don't know. I'll leave it to you."

"All right then, I say, let's go to the Bazooka Club. It's near the Strand and a lot of the RAF go there. It's fun. You'll like it."

Twenty minutes later, they entered the pub-like atmosphere, where the talk was loud and lively. Ken found Anne a seat, then picked his way to the bar and ordered two pints.

It was a spirited, crowded room, mostly connected to the Allied Air Forces. There were Australians, Canadians, South Africans and men from the Free French and Free Polish Air Forces. The men mixed surprisingly well, as they shared their dramatic combat stories and their narrow escapes.

When Ken returned to the table, there were two Royal Air Force pilots sitting with Anne.

"Hello, Yank," the pilot with a mop of blonde hair said. "I'm Jeff, and we've swooped down to whisk your girl away from you. But I think I've stalled out at a thousand feet, and I'm about to crash into the Channel."

The other RAF pilot, a redhead with freckles named Harry, said, "But Anne here told us you are a jolly good fellow and you only have ten missions left to go. So I say, old boy, I think you should buy us a couple of pints, for good luck."

Ken grinned. "I'm not going to leave the two of you here with Anne, while I go back out there and fight that crowd." He jerked a thumb toward the bar. "You get the pints, old boys, and I'll pay for them."

Both pilots laughed. "Good show, Yank," Jeff said.

After introductions, and after they all had a pint before them, the men began exchanging stories.

Ken asked, "What do you fly? Wellingtons?"

Harry said, "No, Jeff and I fly Lancasters."

"I don't know how you guys fly those night missions," Ken said. "I've had to fly two, and it scared the dickens out of me."

"Some nights it's a piece of cake," Jeff said. "Some... well, it's a rough show, I can tell you, especially when the Jerries catch you in their search lights. We're stone blind until we get clear of them."

Anne said, "Let's not talk anymore about the war. Now, Jeff and Harry, where are your girls?"

Jeff scratched his head, while Harry glanced about the room. "They were with us when we got here, but..." he shrugged. "I don't know where they are now. They probably flew off with an Aussie or Canadian. You've got to watch those Canadian blokes. They're like night fighters. They swoop in before you see them, shoot you down and then zip away."

When the air raid siren went off, everyone froze, and then everyone cursed.

Ken pounded the table with a fist. "Dammit!"

"The Jerries are at it again," Harry said.

Harry looked up at the ceiling, angry steel in his eyes. "You bastards! We'll give you some of your own back tomorrow night."

The room burst to life, as the music stopped, the dance floor cleared, and the bar emptied. Ken took Anne's arm and led her through the surging crowd, out the door and onto the street. The bombers were nearly overhead, the booming sound of the anti-aircraft guns blasting, flashing angry red light. Search light beams crisscrossed the sky, catching the shadow of a German bomber here and there, their bombs whistling down.

Anne and Ken made a dash for the underground, just slipping inside as the bombs exploded, rumbling, smashing, splitting open the night.

Although the government had discouraged using the underground as a public shelter, the public used them anyway. They were dry, warm, well-lit and, from inside them, the raids were inaudible.

Anne and Ken found an empty space near a wall and they rested there, Anne leaning her head on Ken's shoulder.

"I had a grand time, Kenneth."

He kissed her hair. "When can I see you again?"

"When can you get away next?"

"I don't know. I'll call you."

"I'll bring Tommy next time. I want him to meet you, and you to meet him. I hope you like him."

"Don't you worry about that. Tommy and I will get along just fine. I know it."

The crowd was huddled and somber. Babies cried. An old man hung his head. A woman knitted, her eyes spilling tears.

Ken took Anne by the shoulders and looked directly into her eyes. "When I finish my missions, I want us to get married. I know you're not sure about it, but once

I'm finished... once I've done what I came here to do, I want us to be together, always. But I have to know. I have to know if you love me. I have to know if you want us to get married."

He studied the look on her face, but he didn't know what it meant. "Do you love me, Anne?"

She turned her eyes up. "You know I love you, Kenneth. You must know. It's just that I'm so very scared, and I don't want to be. I want to be brave."

She turned her head away.

Ken was all smiles. "Then nothing else matters, Anne. If we love each other, then that's all that matters."

She looked at him somberly. "No, Kenneth. It's not so easy. I have to be honest with you. I love you, and it hurts, because we don't know if we're going to be alive or dead tomorrow. You still must fly ten missions, and I don't know if you'll come back to me."

He pulled her into him and wrapped his arms about her. "I will come back, Anne. I will. Now that I know you love me, I promise you, I'll make it through this war and come back to you."

Anne felt the weight of the moment and she pressed her face snugly into his shoulder.

Three hours later, Lieutenant Taylor and Anne Billings had a final kiss before he hailed a cab for Waterloo Station, where he would catch a train back to Ridgewell Aerodrome.

Anne watched him go, feeling both an old heart break and a new heart break, and she stood there, waiting impatiently, for the next time she'd see his face, hear his voice, and feel his lips on hers.

CHAPTER 29
New York City 2008

Constance Crowne and Dr. Jon Miles sat in First Class comfort aboard the British Airways flight to London's Heathrow Airport. While passengers were continuing to board, the friendly flight attendant drifted over and introduced herself.

Constance ordered a glass of champagne and Jon a ginger ale.

After the attendant retreated, Constance turned to Jon. "Why don't you live a little, Jon?" she asked.

Jon flashed her a tight smile. "Before this flight is over, Constance, I'll probably consume at least three gin and tonics."

"Oh, relax. Everything is fine. We'll be in the air soon."

Constance approved of both the champagne, Laurent Perrier Grand Siècle, and the champagne flute it was in. She also approved of the warm towels on silver trays.

"I love this airline," she said. "The British are so civilized."

Jon sipped his ginger ale, casting his nervous eyes about. "Looks like everyone is nearly seated. We should be underway soon."

At 7:45 p.m., the intercom came alive and a flight attendant announced that boarding was complete, at which point the first officer came on the PA and welcomed all aboard.

"Our flight time to London's Heathrow will be six hours and fifty-five minutes, and we will be cruising at thirty-six thousand feet. We expect mostly calm winds, and the flight should be on time."

That's when Constance saw him, and her lips tightened. Alex Fogel had stepped into the plane, along with an official, who was wearing a dark suit and a sober expression. Alex flashed his identification to the nervous flight attendant and quickly shifted his eyes to inspect the first-class passengers.

His icy gaze met Constance's steely gaze, and then he jerked away and went marching up the aisle, glancing about, obviously searching for Anne.

Constance patiently waited for his return.

"Dammit," Jon said at a harsh whisper. "How did he know we were on this plane?"

"Simple," Constance said, coolly. "I told Leon, knowing full well he'd tell his uncle. But I didn't tell Leon everything. Just what he needed to know. I knew nothing would stop Mr. Fogel from his radical purpose."

Alex returned to Constance's seat, glaring down at her. Unintimidated, her eyes were cold and hard on him, her chin set in a challenge.

"What do you want?" she asked, evenly.

He didn't back down. "Don't play games with me, Mrs. Crowne. You know what I want. Where is she? She's not on this plane."

"Who are you looking for?" Constance said innocently.

"Stop the bullshit. I'm not in the mood for it. Where is Anne Billings?"

Constance gave him a withering look of hatred. "I have no idea."

He pointed a threatening finger at her. "I'm warning you. I'll have you thrown off this plane and tossed into jail if you don't tell me where she is, and tell me right now."

Jon bit the inside of his lip, his nervous eyes shifting down and away.

Constance folded her arms; her neck and face burned hot. "How dare you talk to me that way, you puffed up, egotistical, insulting blowhard? If you so much as touch me; if you or anyone else makes the slightest move to have me removed from this airplane, I will call Senator Arlen Paxton's personal number, which I have on my speed dial. He knows I'm on this airplane bound for London. He said I could call him anytime, day or night. You may recall that Senator Paxton is on the Senate Intelligence Committee."

His eyes glided over her, testing and searching for a bluff. He saw none.

With the flight attendant and several passengers looking on uneasily, Constance continued. "Now get out of my sight, or I will file a lawsuit against you for harassment and bodily threats, and anything else I can think of. I have very hungry attorneys just waiting for my call. I will also sue the CIA, including any and all of your superiors, and anyone else my lawyers care to involve. Now, get away from me!"

Anger pulsed at Alex's neck, and his eyes flamed. His voice was low and seething. "I will find her. Wherever she is, I will find her."

"Go to hell," Constance snapped.

Alex turned and stormed off the plane.

Once they were airborne, Jon swiftly ordered a gin and tonic. He ventured a glance at Constance, who was still fuming.

"Well, that went well, I think," Jon said, trying for a joke.

Constance was in no mood for it, and she gave him a side glance of disapproval. "That insufferable bastard! We're not finished with him. He'll hop the first plane to London, and I'm sure he has others looking for Anne too."

"So what do we do now?" Jon asked, his stomach churning.

Constance stared ahead. "Stick to the plan. He'll never find her if I stick to my plan."

When they were at cruising altitude and speed, Jon ordered his second gin and tonic and Constance a second glass of champagne.

While he sipped his drink, Jon stole a glance at Constance. She looked thin, pale and tired. She'd worried herself into lack of sleep with her aggressive plans and hellbent determination to get Anne to safety. Jon admired Constance's obsession, and he knew why she was driven, but she was pushing herself too hard and he hoped she wouldn't break down, not that he could imagine Constance ever breaking down.

Of course, she cared deeply for Anne, and Jon knew, for all of Constance's crusty exterior, the woman was a softy at heart. She fought for animal rights, women's rights, teachers' rights, and civil rights, and she gave generously to the Battered Women's Justice Project.

Jon had first met her in the ER, where he was attending to another young woman who had been attacked and beaten in Central Park. Anne Billings was not the first such woman Constance had taken under her protective wing.

Jon had admired Constance's compassion, generosity and dedication to the battered young woman, and she'd stayed in touch with her. Fortunately, that victim had a family, and they'd come to New York and taken her home to Minnesota.

Jon recalled a conversation they'd had after the girl had left the Intensive Care Unit and was taken to the private room Constance had arranged and paid for.

They were in the hospital lounge, each nursing a cup of coffee. Constance hovered on the edge of tears and rage.

"What kind of monster does that to a young woman? What evil sickness makes them do it?"

Jon had given her a few minutes of professional scrutiny. "Have you been through this before?"

When she'd looked at him, her eyes had burned with fury and pain. That's when she'd told him about Ashley, her murdered daughter.

"They never found Ashley's murderer, not even with DNA testing," Constance had said. "He's still out there somewhere, free, no doubt waiting to attack and kill another woman. Sometimes I go to Central Park at the same time it happened, to the same place where Ashley's body was found. I have a handgun in my purse, and I search, and I walk, and I study all the men's faces as they walk by, or linger in conversation, or sit on a bench reading. I pray to God that the sick bastard who raped and killed my Ashley will try it again and, this time, I'll be there. I'll be there, and I'll pull my gun and shoot him. Shoot him until there are no more bullets. Yes, Dr. Miles. Some people pray for money or for a good job, or for the perfect mate. Do you know what I pray for? I pray for revenge. I pray that one day, I'll find that man and I'll kill him."

As they were making their final approach into Heathrow, Constance turned to Jon, who'd just stirred from a nap. He was surprised when she smiled kindly at him.

"Jon... I've been thinking. I know Anne trusts you and likes you. I know you like her, and maybe you even more than like her. Once I get her to a safe place, why don't you think about asking her to marry you?"

Jon sat up, his sticky eyes opening fully. "Marry?"

"Yes. Anne will need to marry, and it will have to be with someone who is successful and financially stable. Someone she admires. I think you two would be the perfect couple."

He sat stiffly, with a tolerant smile. "Constance, Anne will need time to settle someplace and time to think about her future. I don't think she's going to want to get married right away."

"It doesn't have to be right away."

"And I live and work in New York."

"So you'll move to England and find work. You have friends here who'll help you find the right hospital or private practice."

He shook his head. "You amaze me how you just, I don't know, get everything arranged in your head and then just go for it."

"Why not? I know you care for Anne, and you know I have the greatest admiration and respect for you."

"Thank you for that and, yes, I do care for Anne and, yes, she is someone I would like to consider marrying. All I'm saying is that there are many things to work out before there is any discussion of marriage. First and foremost, we must make sure she is safe, comfortable and healthy."

"And we will. That goes without saying. Frankly, Jon, she will need a man. She's a young woman with a woman's needs and wants, and she is quite alone in this world. I don't think it will take long for her to realize that she is in love with you."

"You flatter me."

"No, I'm a realist and I know she feels safe and secure with you. She's told me as much."

Jon rested back in his seat with a little sigh. "You still haven't told me where she is and where you plan to hide her."

"I'll tell you when it's time to tell you, Jon. Right now, the fewer people who know, the better."

Constance half-hooded her eyes and lowered her voice, but it still had an edge to it. "As I said earlier, I don't think Alex Fogel is the type to stop searching. I may have to find a way to *make* him stop."

Jon looked at her, gently startled. "What are you saying?"

Constance made little nods. "Excluding present company, Jon, most of the time I'm not so fond of men. All I'm saying is that I'm not so fond of Alex Fogel and I will not—no, not ever—allow Anne to be taken by him, to be locked up, prodded, studied and God knows what. All I'm saying is, if I have to stop him, I *will* stop him."

CHAPTER 30
England 2008

Anne Billings sat alone in one of the nine seats of the Citation X, a private jet en route to Farnborough Airport in Hampshire, England. She stared out into the darkness, having been recently told by the friendly but formal male flight attendant that they were flying at thirty-five thousand feet and they'd arrive in Farnborough in about two hours.

She'd eaten an hour ago, a deluxe ham and cheese sandwich, with crisps, a delicious pickle, and a strong pot of English Breakfast tea. The food had relaxed her just enough so that she was able to steal a twenty-minute nap before jarring awake, recalling Tommy's apple cheeks and Lieutenant Kenneth Taylor's warm, penetrating eyes. They'd seemed so close, as if she could reach out and touch Tommy's cheek, as if Kenneth were reaching out to take her hand.

Her mind speeded up and her thoughts became erratic and worried. Constance told her everything would be fine, and Anne had no reason to doubt her but, once again, here she was depending on Constance to help her get out of the mess she was in.

Back in New York, twenty-five minutes after they'd started for Kennedy Airport, Constance had instructed the driver to pull into a mall where a separate limo was waiting. After Constance had ushered Anne into the second limo, she explained that Anne would be flying to England from another airport, Teterboro Airport in Teterboro, New Jersey. She said not to worry, that everything had been taken care of.

Constance had added, "You'll be the only passenger on the plane, so don't worry. You'll fly nonstop to England and land at a private airport in Hampshire, England, and I've pre-cleared your flight with customs and immigration to ensure a smooth arrival."

Anne could only stare, her head spinning, her senses overloaded.

"Now listen carefully, Anne. When you arrive, a private car will be waiting for you. I have arranged a place for you to stay that is private and safe. I'll join you there as soon as I'm sure I'm not being followed."

Constance had taken Anne's hand, smiling tenderly. "Don't you worry about a thing. I won't let anything happen to you. You'll be back in your own country soon. You'll be home again."

Relaxed in her seat, studying her reflection in the oval airplane window, Anne kept playing back Constance's words, "You'll be back in your own country. You'll be home again."

The words were comforting and yet disturbing. Her own country? Home? But it was 2008, not 1944. She was about to arrive in a strange new world, where nothing would look the same or be the same. Would anyone she knew in 1944 still be alive?

Anne lost herself in longing and imagination as she considered the odd panorama of her life. And then she thought of her Dad, who had got along in life by listening and watching. He'd been a mild man who had never— not once—shouted at her or struck her. He was an inward man, a man who kept much to himself, and Anne now realized that she'd hadn't really known him.

Working as a laborer at the East End docklands, his satisfaction had come from hard work, a quiet family life, and smoking his pipe in the evening while he read the newspaper or listened to the radio. He'd comforted and flattered and treasured his wife, and theirs had been a true marriage of love and mutual respect, the kind of love that everyone had admired, including Anne.

Over the years of watching her parents' playful hands finding each other, their flirty jokes, and their secret code of lusty glances, Anne had developed what had become a simple set of rules about marriage: find a good man like Dad and be his loving, caring wife like Mom. But it hadn't turned out that way, almost from the beginning.

Flying at thirty-five thousand feet above the Atlantic Ocean, Anne had a troubling epiphany. It was the distance, and the height, and the time and the year. She continued to stare at her reflection in the jet window, and she thought hard about her marriage to Basil, a marriage she'd regretted a few months after the ceremony. She had never admitted that regret to herself, nor to anyone else. It was a regret that had carried an unspoken pain and guilt.

Basil had a temper—something he hadn't revealed to her, or something she hadn't noticed while they dated. Within only weeks of the ceremony, he'd begun shouting at her, a red-faced kind of shout for small infractions: dinner wasn't ready on time; her ironing was careless; the flat wasn't clean. She'd passed it off as his nerves over the war, and she'd forgiven him. He wasn't a bad sort, just worried. And he was her husband for always.

He'd slapped her more than once when she'd tried to defend herself, or when she'd tried to offer an explanation. How could she have ever admitted to her mom, or to any of her friends, that she and Basil seemed to be growing apart instead of drawing closer together, as a man and his wife are supposed to do? And their love-making had often been rough, painful and abrupt. Sometimes, she'd felt lonely and dirty afterwards. No, she couldn't share that with anyone, certainly not her mom.

And then in July 1940, the Battle of Britain began, and Basil was gone, flying missions nearly every day until his death on August 12, 1940, when he was shot down over the English Channel.

When she'd received the news, she'd been knocked literally speechless, and she remained that way for more than two weeks. She was also pregnant with Tommy.

Back home with her parents, Anne didn't sleep well for weeks after Basil's death, her guilt and her mad confusion knotting her muscles, shrinking her stomach, and battering her spirit. The only thing that had saved her were her kind and loving parents. It was they who'd nursed her back to health. And when the bombs fell, they all ran for the shelter, Anne terrified she'd lose Tommy.

After Tommy was born, a "cold strangeness" had filled her; not quite depression; not quite sickness; not quite rage, but parts of all three. Months later, it was her Dad who finally took her by the shoulders and sat her down for a frank conversation. He said, "Anne, make yourself useful. Get out of this house and go find something to do. You're no good for little Tommy when you drag on, day after day, in a mood. Go find a job."

She applied for and got the job at Bletchley Park, but she'd hesitated before accepting it. What about Tommy? What about her baby? How could she leave her baby? What kind of mother was she to leave him when he was but one year old?

Again, it had been her Dad who'd given her wise and soothing counsel. "Your mother and I will look after little Tommy. Don't you have a care about that now, Annie. You go out into this battling world and do what you have to do."

"But how can I leave him? I love him with all my heart."

"Your heart is broken now, and these are not normal times, Annie. You've been broken by the sacrifice of your husband and the birth of your son in the midst of this hellish war. Your heart is in need of mending. You go and work for a time. It will be the best thing for you, and it will help heal you. Work is good for body and soul and, anyway, with the men gone, your country needs smart women like you in its hour of trial."

Anne listened, pondering how she had lost her way so completely.

"You come home when you can, Annie. You're not so far. When you do come home for your visits, Tommy will be here, and he will hold his love for you. There's no doubt about that. No child ever forgets the smell, and the look, and the touch of his own mum. Don't you worry about it none, Annie. Tommy will be surrounded by love here, with us, who love him."

Anne had been terribly conflicted but, in the end, she went to work at Bletchley, returning home whenever she could. Two years later, she couldn't take it any longer, and she left to be with her son, promising to make up for the time she'd been away.

And then they'd been trapped in an air raid and Tommy was gone. Was it God's own punishment meted out to her for leaving Tommy?

Anne was jarred from her memories when the flight attendant approached, with a little bow and a half smile.

"We are making our final approach. Is there anything else I can bring you, Ms. Watson?"

She shook her head, the old memories refusing to recede. "No... Thank you."

"As I said when you boarded, a car will be waiting for you, and all customs and immigration have been cleared, so you can proceed directly to the awaiting car."

When he returned to the attendant's station, Anne thought, *What happened to Mum and Dad? Did they survive the bombings?*

While the jet's red and white landing lights flooded the area, Anne descended the airstairs to the tarmac, under cloudy skies and a forty-one-degree temperature. She saw a tall, fit man loom out of the foggy mist and approach, wearing a black flat cap and dark rain coat, swinging an umbrella.

He drew up, removed his cap, and offered a head bow. "Miss Watson, I am Reese Patrick, estate manager."

Anne noticed his Irish accent.

"If you will be so good as to accompany me to the awaiting car, we'll be off. Pardon me while I get your luggage and load it into the auto."

Anne hesitated, feeling a chilly mist on her face. He was an imposing man, with short silver hair and stony features, but friendly eyes.

"Has Constance Crowne arranged this?" Anne asked, hesitating.

"Yes, Miss Watson. She has arranged your travel as well as your forthcoming accommodations. Mrs. Crowne will not contact you for a number of days, due to security issues. She will communicate with you when she is certain it is prudent to do so."

After Reese retrieved her suitcase, she followed him to the black town car, feeling as though she were an actress in a spy picture. She half expected to see Trevor Howard, a British actor she loved, materialize from the misty darkness and tell her she was in grave danger, and that she'd better make a run for it.

Underway, Reese glanced at Anne through the rearview mirror, noticing she sat stiffly, her eyes moving. "Are you quite comfortable, then, Miss Watson?"

"Yes... thank you. How far is it to our destination?"

"About thirty kilometers."

In thick darkness and a fine rain, Reese Patrick drove the car along a quiet, winding road, through patches of wooly, rolling fog. While they plunged deeper into the strange, obscuring world of 2008 England, Anne gazed out the window, feeling as though the night were alive with nefarious spirits and alert, crouching CIA agents.

Anne's breath rose, got caught in anxiety, then was released in staccato bursts. God, she'd never been so scared and so lost. Where was she going? What would she do? She couldn't hide forever. She'd have to find work and begin a new life. She'd have to find ways to adjust and melt into this modern world, and she'd have to find a way to pay Constance back for everything she'd done for her. Constance had literally saved her life and she would never forget it. If it took the rest of her life, Anne would find a way to repay her.

"Courage, Anne," she said to herself, at a whisper, working to steady her breath, recalling what her Dad used to say during air raids. "Let's get ahold of ourselves now, have courage, and stop all the mind-racing tittle-tattle. We'll get through this right enough."

The car left the main road, turning left, motoring up a long drive toward a large house that emerged in shadowy light.

A great mystery, naked and unguarded, was waiting for her and she would meet it, whatever it was, with dogged courage. That's how her parents had raised her, and that's what World War Two had taught her.

CHAPTER 31
England 2008

Constance knew she was being watched. She'd spotted Alex's reflection in a shop window. Maybe she should have been unnerved and on edge, but there was something about the game that appealed to her sense of adventure; her need for a challenge; her hatred of Alex Fogel, and all men like him. But Constance knew that however her mind calculated and plotted, it couldn't compete with Alex's professional mind, which worked with experience and proven instinct.

Constance was staying in London at the five-star luxury hotel, The May Fair, in a one-bedroom suite, complete with a spacious lounge, kitchen, and dining area.

She'd spent her first three days Christmas shopping at upscale shops, mostly for Anne; visiting the National Gallery; and, with Jon Miles, attending a production of Renee Fleming as Violetta in *La Traviata* at the Royal Opera House.

Jon was also staying at The May Fair in a modest room on a lower floor. He'd spent his time at the hotel gym, taking calls from colleagues in New York, and visiting a friend in Her Majesty's Diplomatic Service. He lived a short distance away in Mayfair, an upscale district of elegant Georgian townhouses, exclusive hotels, and gourmet restaurants.

Jon had been generously wining and dining his friend, telling him about Anne without divulging her entire, astonishing story. He was seeking a practical method to arrange British citizenship for Anne, given her unique circumstances.

It had been part of Constance's plan to split her and Jon up, thus stretching Alex Fogel's spying resources, which had to be modest, at best.

Upon her arrival, she'd called Senator Paxton. Unfortunately, the Senator had not been as accommodating as he'd first let on.

"I don't get involved with the brass in intelligence if I don't have to, Constance," he'd said over the phone. "They don't trust outsiders, and they don't like politicians sticking their noses into their business. However, I did put in a call to a contact I have there. I won't mention his name. He said he'd look into it, which probably means he won't do a damned thing. My advice to you is that if this agent fellow shows up, bluff him. Tell him to get the hell away or I'll have his superiors on him so fast it will make his head swim."

Constance was not encouraged. She'd already done that, and it hadn't worked.

On Thursday, December 11, Constance lay sprawled on the deep leather couch of her lounge, sipping a glass of champagne, a slow burn of impatience beginning to rise. She had not left her suite that day, and she longed to talk to Anne, but she couldn't chance it. She didn't know for sure, but she speculated that Alex could monitor her cell phone calls and, even if he couldn't, she didn't feel comfortable calling.

Constance had received a confirmation that Anne had arrived safely at the quaint and lovely mill house in Hampshire and that she had settled in comfortably, although Reese Patrick wrote that she was jittery.

The communication had been prearranged with Mr. Patrick. He'd sent a written confirmation to the Royal Opera House, to a contact there, his sister. Constance had been handed the envelope as she retrieved her tickets at the box office. At least in the short term, that would be the method of communication.

Constance would be returning to the opera that night, with a letter she'd written to Anne, hoping to receive one from Anne in return. It was Constance's plan to wait Alex out. After all, how long could he stay in London? He couldn't be forever on vacation. How many personal leave days did he have? Didn't he have a real job to return to? Didn't he have to answer to a boss? How long could he hold out? That was the question.

When Jon arrived and entered Constance's lounge, she handed him a glass of champagne and eagerly awaited his citizenship news.

Jon settled in a chair and Constance returned to the couch.

"What have you got for me? Were you able to learn anything?" Constance asked, her eyes glowing and eager.

An extravagant vase of fresh flowers bloomed between them. Jon rose and slid the arrangement to the left of the glass coffee table, but he didn't return to the chair. He stood, pondering.

"Well?" Constance asked, impatient. "What did this Alan Welton say?"

"Do you trust me enough to tell me where Anne is and who is looking after her? I've asked twice and both times you've changed the subject. So, do you trust me or not?"

Constance's voice was elaborately casual. "It's not about trust, Jon. I trust you. It's just that the fewer people who know where she is, the better. Anne is staying at a house where Charles and I once stayed. We had a family reunion there a year or two before his death, and we both loved it. I thought it the perfect hiding place for Anne. I stayed in touch with the estate agent and she was able to recommend a former military man to look after Anne. He is the manager for the estate and also one of the owners. It all worked out rather nicely. Now, what have you learned from your diplomat friend?"

Jon's gaze wandered. "We already knew that a person has to have lived in the UK for at least three years before filing an application for citizenship."

"Yes... and? Stop stalling, Jon. What else?"

"Alan said he might be able to shave a year off that, but no more. I tried to argue that the situation was extraordinary. I suggested that, if he knew the entire story, then he, or someone he knew, would probably grant a passport and citizenship ASAP. Well, of course, he wanted to know what was so extraordinary."

Jon paused, took a nervous sip of the champagne and continued. "As we speculated, he wants to meet Anne."

Jon looked at Constance soberly. "Alan's married, but it's not a happy marriage, and he does see other women. I'm sure he'd fall head-over-heels for Anne."

Constance rose to her feet and cursed. "He can't be trusted then. So, that's that. I wish I knew someone in this country who had some power."

"I almost told Alan everything, out of desperation."

"I'm glad you didn't. All we need is the British Secret Service elbowing in on us, asking questions. We have enough problems."

Jon sighed. "Look, Constance, Alan said he could manage to get her a legit passport, as long as she's not a terrorist or some anarchist. I say we let him do it and then have Anne stay out of sight for a couple of years. Then we can apply for her citizenship. As I see it now, it's the best way."

Constance shook her head. "I don't think she'll last that long. She'll go stir-crazy and put herself at risk, and Alex Fogel will track her down by then."

Jon shrugged. "So, what do we do?"

"I don't know. I've been looking at this from all angles and it's stumped me. Believe it or not, I'm thinking of putting myself out there, in British high society, to see if I can meet someone."

"Meet someone? I'm not following you."

"I need to meet a powerful man who can help us."

Jon looked at her, incredulous. "Are you serious?"

"Yes, I'm serious. What? You don't think I'm desirable enough to attract a man?"

"Of course you are, but... it sounds a little desperate."

"And we are desperate. So, desperate times demand desperate measures. How does the expression go?

Fortune seldom favors the faint of heart. My husband knew some wealthy people over here who were connected to the political set. I'll begin by contacting them and then see if I can blunder into some ostentatious party, where I can play the role of the lonely, widowed American."

Jon studied her, carefully. "Are you really that dedicated to Anne?"

There was a sharp gleam of conviction in her eyes. "You bet I am. And, yes, I know what you're thinking. You believe that Anne is a substitution for Ashley and I'm over-reacting." Constance moved close to Jon and looked him directly into the eyes.

"Yes, Jon... I *am* over-reacting because in my soul, I love Anne. She's scared and hurting, and if it weren't for me, she would be completely alone in this world. And Alex Fogel, or someone like him, or worse, would have grabbed her by now, and God only knows what would have happened to her. I took her on and, when I did, I vowed to see this through. I vowed to help her anyway I could, and that's exactly what I'm going to do."

Their eyes held while the silence lengthened.

"Are you going to ask her to marry you?" Constance asked, bluntly.

Jon turned and walked away, setting his glass down, keeping his back to her. "Anne is not ready for marriage. She's confused and, I don't know, up in the air."

"Then catch her, bring her down to Earth and hold her. Love her. Help her. She will soon say, 'yes.' When you're married, she'll become an American citizen, and it will throw Alex Fogel off-balance."

"And where will we get married? Here?"

"Of course here, and the sooner the better."

Jon faced Constance, his expression conflicted. "I've been thinking a lot about this, and maybe I don't want to marry Anne. Maybe there's just too much baggage."

"Baggage?" Constance asked, insulted. "What an awful and terrible thing to say."

"You know what I mean. I like Anne, yes. Perhaps I could even fall in love with her, but I'm not ready to toss my life up into the air—my career, my family, and everything I've worked for—to go on the run with Anne, a troubled woman who wants to return to her real life in 1944."

There was a long pause, while Constance processed Jon's words. "She can't ever return, Jon, you know that. You must help her realize that, and you must help her forget the past."

Jon shook his head. "Did you hear me? Did you hear what I just said? I'm not going to have my life choreographed and arranged by you, Constance. You think you have all the answers for everybody. Well, not for me, you don't. I'm not ready to sprint off to some country estate and declare my undying love for Anne. Face it, Constance. Anne will always long for her own time, and who wouldn't? She's a woman of that time, not this, and she'll never be truly happy here. She'll always be wanting to go home."

Constance lifted her head, commandingly, her voice strong, her spirit undeterred. "Fine, Jon. If you feel that way, then you should leave England and return to New York."

Jon pocketed his hands and gazed toward the ceiling. He breathed out a long sigh. "I know what you're going to do. You're going to find Anne a British husband, aren't you?"

"I'll do whatever I have to do to keep Anne safe and happy. In many ways, it will be easier if you leave. Anne is so pretty and smart. It won't take her any time at all to meet and marry a man with status and money. And she'll become a British citizen right away. All problems solved. Thank you very much, Dr. Jon Miles."

Jon lowered his frosty stare on her. "God help you, Constance, and God help Anne. She's going to need it."

Jon turned on his heels and left the room.

CHAPTER 32
England 2008

Anne couldn't take it any longer. She felt like a caged animal, trapped in old English style and beauty. Fairview Meadows was a three-story, red brick mill house with a red tile roof, frequented by fly fishermen who came to fish in the nearby River Anton.

There were six reception rooms on the ground floor, along with a kitchen and a large breakfast room with French doors opening onto a lavishly manicured garden, with hedgerows, fountains and birdbaths.

On the second floor were five double bedrooms, four bathrooms and a nursery. Above that were three additional bedrooms, and one was Anne's room. It had a spectacular view of the garden, a sloping meadow and distant woodlands. From another window, Anne could see an old carriage house, a curving river, and a section of a two-lane road that led to a village, two kilometers away.

On Friday, December 12, Anne left the house in a quick, cold wind, searching for Reese Patrick. She found him returning from the carriage house, where the cars were kept. Reese wore a herringbone tweed coat and glossy brown boots.

She drew up to him, breathless, her cheeks red from the wind.

Before she could speak, Reese put two fingers to his tweed flat cap and smiled, showing crooked front teeth.

"Good morning, Miss Watson. Will you be needing anything?"

Her voice was edged and anxious. "Mr. Patrick... Can you drive me into London? What I mean to say is, not for a shopping trip or anything like that, but just as a kind of tour of the city?"

He looked at her, long and serious. "Now, I don't think that would be the good and right thing to do, Miss Watson. Mrs. Crowne would surely counsel against it."

"Please, Mr. Patrick. We could do a quick drive through, and I won't leave the car. I'm sure no one will be the wiser or know I'm there. I must escape this lovely jail and see London again. It's the reason I came all this way."

His staring eyes looked beyond her. "Miss Watson, Mrs. Crowne's instructions to me were to keep you here and to watch over you."

"And you will, sir. I'll be seated behind you with nowhere else to go."

And then she turned her face aside so he couldn't read it. She intended to burst from the car and stroll through London, exploring and searching for the place where the bomb had blown her into another time and place.

He scratched his head above his left ear. "All right, Miss Watson, but I must tell you, this will be the one and only time I'll put you at risk and go against Mrs. Crowne's wishes."

His eyes were slitted, inspecting her.

AS THEY DROVE PAST wealthy estates, south-flowing rivers and areas of downland and marsh, Anne was thoughtful, her mind bringing out impressions and recollections. While working at Bletchley, she'd learned that, somewhere in this area, there had been a finishing school for agents, operated by the Special Operations Executive or the SOE. There had also been a Royal Navy harbor at Portsmouth and an army camp at Aldershot. Now that her full memory had returned, these memories seemed fresh and immediate, because she'd left 1944 only a few weeks before.

As they crossed the Thames at Westminster Bridge, entering London, Anne's heart nearly seized up. The foot traffic was heavy; the car traffic was knotted with red, double-decker buses and taxis. A young woman sat playing an accordion, an old French tune Anne recognized but couldn't name.

And then a strange, unnamable fear washed over her as she took in the changed skyline. There was the Palace of Westminster and Big Ben and St. Paul's, but what was that gigantic Ferris wheel doing there, and where were the industrialized sites along the Thames?

As they drove on, towers in various shapes and sizes rose up, glinting in the early afternoon sun. It was a 3-D London in a futuristic world; a London feverishly recrafted into an expression of soaring, gleaming-glass dominance and surreal shapes, all super-imposed on the old London she remembered.

A vision of the past seized and startled her. Where was the bomb damage? Where were the broken walls, the damaged chimneys, the piles of rubble and scattered bricks in the streets? Where were the war-weary, slouching survivors, picking through debris, searching for buried bodies or precious keep-sakes or furniture scattered helter-skelter?

Where were the sturdy, unrelenting people, the ubiquitous soldiers in uniforms, the bell-ringing ambulance sirens, the barrage balloons, the Spitfires and Hurricane fighters soaring across the sky? Where was the thick smoke that hung over the heart of Britain after the German bombers had bombed through the night?

At a stop light, Reese swiveled around. "Is there any place that you particularly wish to see, Miss?"

Anne didn't answer him. When her vision of the past cleared, she sat in a stupor of shock, unable to speak, as this new and unrecognizable London unraveled all around her, striking her senses with a violence she could have never expected.

The war was gone—of course it was gone—because she was living in 2008, not 1944. It was a good thing, wasn't it? Wasn't it a blessing that the war had ended a long time ago and there were no more bombs, no more violence, destruction and death?

Anne felt cold, and she hugged herself, feeling the chaos of emotions beat through her.

Concerned, Reese glanced at her through his rearview mirror and saw that she'd gone white, her face blank with shock.

"Are you quite all right, Miss Watson?"

When they approached Trafalgar Square, Anne sat up, bolt erect, her eyes wide and searching. On reflex, she pointed and blurted out, "That's it!"

Reese jerked a look toward the square. "What is it, Miss?"

"Kenneth and I met here, at Trafalgar Square, in 1944. Kenneth was a pilot... he flew a bomber out of the Ridgeway Aerodrome. When he was on leave, we often met over there, between those two bronze lions. The area along the Strand and Trafalgar Square was always crowded, so we'd meet here, at the statue of Horatio Nelson, on the square, between those two lions, one on each side of the admiral."

Reese stared, trying to understand.

Anne's face fell into melancholy. "It hasn't changed so much... Not at all. It was so long ago now... So long... And yet, I remember, don't I, like it was only yesterday."

Reese shifted uncomfortably in his seat.

Anne shut her eyes, unable to take anything else in. There were so many places she wanted to see and remember: The Ritz, Piccadilly Square, Hyde Park, but she couldn't face them and the old memories. She didn't have the stomach for it.

Anne lost track of time, and when she opened her eyes, they were driving through Charing Cross. Despite the tightness in her throat, she managed to say, "Please take me to Stratford. I want to go home to Stratford. Do you know where it is?"

"Yes, Miss Watson. It's about ten kilometers from here to East London."

Anne braced herself for what was to come, staring out into the afternoon sun, watching the modern world blur by, not wanting to see it, not wanting to acknowledge a changed city that was no longer familiar; that was no longer her home.

To fill the anxious silence, Reese began to banter away. "About Stratford, I read something interesting in the paper. Because of the financial crisis, they're having difficulty raising funds on the commercial markets for the construction of the 2012 Olympic Village. Some politician said that Stratford is a forgotten part of London, and they need the Olympics. He said building hotels and shopping centers, cinemas and a casino would boost its economy and help the entire city. What do you think, Miss... I mean since you come from there?"

"Forgotten part of London?" Anne asked, distracted, struggling to understand and follow the conversation.

Reese continued. "The concern is over the infrastructure. They question whether Stratford can cope."

As they entered Stratford, Anne was rattled and miserable. "Where are the row houses and the old neighborhoods?" she said at a sad whisper. "Everything is gone... changed."

As Reese was driving by St John's Church, Anne shouted for him to stop, and he pulled over. It was the main parish church in Stratford, standing on Stratford Broadway, the main thoroughfare.

Anne gazed out the car window, clouds of anxiety in her eyes as she viewed the gray brick structure and the three-stage tower. She felt as though she were a ghost who'd risen from the dead.

Anne spoke aloud, in a haunted voice. "During the war, the church crypt served as an air raid shelter. It was damaged by German bombs... Yes, I remember that, and all the windows were blown out. Mrs. Toomey and her daughter were killed just over there, by those trees... but the trees had been blasted away. There was a wrought-iron fence there then and a lovely flower garden."

Anne's voice was strange, and low, and honest. Reese had a chill come over him, and he removed his eyes from the rearview mirror.

Anne inhaled a deep breath and looked about. "I don't even know where our house was. Nothing's left. It's all gone. Everything is completely altered."

Reese had a thought that made him wary and uneasy. Perhaps the reason Constance Crowne wanted Anne sequestered and protected in that grand house in Hampshire had something to do with the young woman's mind. Is that why Mrs. Crowne wanted the pretty Anne kept under wraps? It made sense to him, yes. Anne Watson's mind had twisted on her, and she'd gone a little balmy.

Did she think she was living in 1944, or had lived in 1944? Mrs. Crowne had told him that Anne had been ill and needed rest. Now it all added up, and Reese cursed himself for agreeing to drive her to London. It had been a bad mistake; the mistake of an amateur.

Reese twisted around. "We should return to Hampshire, Miss Watson."

Anne's mind scurried for a hiding place. She couldn't take much more, or she'd go completely mad. But where could she go? She didn't have a home in this time, and she didn't fit into this modern world.

In a small voice she said, "Where can I go? Where? Please get me away from here. I can't bear it any longer."

Reese saw her features falling apart, her eyes filling with tears.

"All right, then, don't you have a worry, Miss. We'll start back straightaway," Reese said, firmly. "You'll be fine once you have yourself a rest, Miss Watson."

As they drove away, Anne leaned forward. "Can we go by way of Hyde Park? I must see it again... I have to."

"It's a bit out of the way, Miss."

"Please..."

Later, when Anne's cell phone rang, Reese tensed up. Through the rearview mirror, he observed Anne reach into her purse and draw out her phone.

"Anne, it's Constance. I'm going to be brief. I need to speak to you about some things, so I'll join you in Hampshire tomorrow."

Anne was quiet.

"Anne... are you there?"

"Yes."

"I'm going to take my time getting there, in case I'm followed. Are you all right?"

Anne stared ahead, speaking in a bland voice. "Yes... I'm feeling a little shaky but..."

"... What's the matter?" Constance asked, interrupting. "You don't sound like yourself."

"I'm in London, Constance. I just visited Stratford."

"What? What did you just say?" Constance asked with alarm. "Did you say you're in London?"

"Yes, we're stuck in traffic, near Hyde Park. There seems to be an incident ahead. We're not moving."

"Dammit! Anne... What on earth are you doing in London?"

"I asked Mr. Patrick to drive me. Don't be upset. We're returning to Hampshire as soon as the traffic clears."

Constance held back anger. "Anne, give the phone to Mr. Patrick."

Reluctantly, Anne obeyed, with a face of apology to Reese as she did so.

While Constance shouted at him, Reese apologized and worked to smooth the situation. Anne's attention was drawn outside. There were dozens of police about, waving people away. A cordon was being expanded near Hyde Park.

As the past and present collided, memories clashed, and old conversations clattered in. On a whim, Anne shoved the door open and climbed out. She heard Reese's urgent voice calling out after her, but she ignored him and started off.

She drew up to a policeman and asked him what was going on.

"Both the north and south bank of the Serpentine are closed off," he said, glancing about.

Anne knew that the Serpentine was a vast recreational lake in Hyde Park, close to Kensington Palace. She and Kenneth had walked the area several times on their strolls through the park in 1944, and her father had brought her there when she was a little girl.

"Why is it closed off?" Anne asked.

"They discovered an unexploded World War Two bomb—a fifty pounder, I was told. Specialist officers have been called to the scene to diffuse it. They said it's close to the Serpentine Lake, near the Pavilion. You should step away now, Miss. We're evacuating this entire area for safety's sake."

"Did you say it was a World War Two bomb?" Anne asked.

"Yes, ma'am. It's not the first, and it won't be the last. A few months back, a five-hundred-pound bomb was found near Soho's Dean Street by construction workers. They cordoned-off that area as well. My dad's a bit of a history buff, and he told me that during the Second World War, German air raids dropped more than twelve thousand metric tons of bombs on London, so some are bound to still be hidden in the ground and the streets. Step back now, Miss, and keep a safe distance."

Anne turned away, her eyes cool, direct and intense. In a sudden burst of wind that blew her red beret from her head, Anne heard the call of her time, 1944.

She jerked her attention to the park, feeling the urge to run, hearing the steady drone of airplanes approaching from the east, a formation of German He-111s, twin-engine, medium bombers poised to bomb London.

In her head, she heard a still, small voice whisper, "It's time to make it right again, Anne. Go!"

An air raid warden blew his shrill whistle, and Anne heard him shout, "Step lively, now! Step lively!"

She heard Tommy's terrified cries. "Mummy... Are they going to drop bombs on us?"

Reese boiled from the car as horns blared all around him, as traffic stalled, as tempers flared. Whipping his head from side to side, he searched for Anne. But he was too late.

She'd bolted away, breaking through a crowd and entering the park. Two startled policemen spotted her and shouted at her to stop.

But she didn't stop. Hearing the echo of war all about her, she dashed off toward Serpentine Lake.

CHAPTER 33
England 2008

Constance left The May Fair Hotel just as the afternoon sun was eclipsed by a dark cloud. The air was chilly, but the mood festive, the Christmas lights glittering, the streets and stores wrapped in the many colors, styles and moods of the season.

She started toward Hyde Park, heading northeast on Stratton Street. With lengthening strides, she turned onto Berkeley Street, not bothering to glance back to see if Alex Fogel was following her. Getting to Anne as fast as possible was her priority. She'd deal with Alex when the time came. Her .38 caliber handgun was tucked snuggly into her designer bag and, if he got in her way, she wouldn't hesitate to brandish it, if it came to that.

Constance was certain he wouldn't risk creating a scene in a foreign country, and surely he knew, by this point, that she didn't give a damn. She'd even welcome it, pointing her gun at him with any and all to see. She had nothing to lose but money for legal counsel, and maybe a few hours in a London police station. On the other hand, he would embarrass the agency, lose his job, be a laughingstock, and never work in intelligence again.

When she reached Park Lane, she called Reese. He was out searching for Anne.

"Is there any sign of her?" Constance asked, urgency in her voice.

"No, Mrs. Crowne. They've got the entire area blocked off. I spoke to a policeman, explaining that she'd entered the park, but he refused to let me search for her."

"All right. I should be there in a few minutes. Did the policeman say where the bomb is?"

"Near the Serpentine Pavilion, in one of the gardens. He said a park attendant found the bomb."

Constance weaved her way past dog walkers, skipping little girls holding hands, and tourists. Just as she was about to enter the park, near a sidewalk artist's display, she heard a voice that chilled her.

"They won't let you in, Mrs. Crowne."

She whirled about to see Alex Fogel standing a few feet away. A shadow crossed her face. "Get the hell away from me."

He pointed. "See the cops, Mrs. Crowne? Neither one of us will get in now. And who knows where Anne went? She's scared to death, running like a stampeding wild animal. But don't worry, they'll catch her."

She glared at him. "What is it with you? Just leave her alone. She needs friends. She needs help so she can adapt to this time. The last thing she needs is you, and others like you, making her life miserable."

Alex wasn't moved. "She'll have the life of her dreams, and I'll make sure she gets all the professional help she needs, all the money she could ever want, and a house she could never dream of. On top of all that, she'll give us insight into things *we* never could have dreamed of."

He stepped closer. "Anne Billings, or Watson, or whatever you want to call her, has actually time traveled, Constance. It's incredible, and impossible, and I'm not going to let her get away. All I want is for her to share her experiences with us. Perhaps we can even learn what actually caused a break in time, and how she time traveled from East London in 1944 to Central Park in 2008. No, Mrs. Crowne, I can't, and I won't, let her go."

Constance was snaking her hand into her handbag, feeling for the grip of the gun, when she heard an explosion, a rumbling roar that shook the ground. There were screams. People dived for cover; ducked away or pointed, faces tense with shock.

In horror, Constance swung around to see an orange fireball shoot up into the air, forming an ugly, dark, mushroom cloud.

Constance screamed out, "NOooo!" and then darted off, breaking through a line of stunned policemen who had turned to see the explosion. Alex tore off after her, the policemen suddenly alert, breaking away, giving chase, waving their arms and shouting for them to stop.

TWO DAYS LATER, CONSTANCE sat slumped in a chair in her May Fair Hotel room, with the curtains pulled and the lights out. A silver wine bucket was stuffed with an upside-down champagne bottle, and on the floor beside the chair was an empty champagne glass, toppled over on the carpet where she'd dropped it.

The darkness, and the wind outside, and the rain striking the windows, were all full of Anne's voice. Constance heard the many conversations they'd shared; heard Anne's soft British accent and the smooth tone of her words. Most of all, Constance heard her own words echoing back at her: the promise that she'd protect Anne.

"Nothing's going to happen to you," Constance said aloud, in a low, self-mocking tone; in a slurring voice filled with loathing.

The champagne had dulled her, and loosened her, and made her mean. "You good-for-nothing bitch," Constance shouted. "You lost her... You lost her, just like you lost Ashley... Gone!"

Constance had called the police every hour, on the hour, to ask if they'd learned anything new.

"Have you found her?" Constance demanded. "You must have found her by now."

"No, Mrs. Crowne," the deep, impatient voice said on the end of the phone. "I've told you, if we learn anything new at all, I'll ring you straightaway."

Sitting in the chair, a dull weariness came over her. She listened to the storm outside and felt pain wrap itself around her pounding heart and squeeze it, like the fingers of a fat hand, tightening, applying pressure.

It was that damned bomb exploding that tormented her. That freak accident. How could something like that happen?

With a struggle of effort, she pushed up on unsteady legs, her temples beating with pounding blood.

That tall, irritable police inspector had told her he'd received reports from two policemen, who had both seen a woman running toward the area where the bomb specialists were working to diffuse the bomb. After it accidently detonated, killing three men and injuring four others, the woman was nowhere to be found. They also didn't find a woman's body. Since that time, Anne Watson had not been located in any hospital, airport, train station… or anywhere else.

Later, the police inspector informed her that another policeman had reported seeing a woman blasted into the air when the bomb detonated but, when pressed, he said he wasn't absolutely sure.

Her cell phone rang. Constance moved toward it, picked it up and saw the call was from Jon Miles. He was home in New York, and he'd been calling for two days, but she hadn't answered or called him back.

Now she answered, annoyed. "Jon…" she said flatly.

"For God's sake, Constance, why haven't you called me?"

"Because I didn't want to. Because I don't want to talk to anyone."

"All right, just tell me if Anne has been found."

"In short, no. She's just… vanished."

"I can't believe it," Jon said, sadly.

"Well, believe it, or don't believe it. Maybe we both dreamed up the whole thing. Maybe Anne was some hallucination. Maybe she was swindling us. Maybe the joke's on us. What the hell do I know about anything."

"You know she wasn't swindling us."

Constance slumped back down into the chair, dropping her head forward. Her voice fell into sorrow. "All I know, Jon, is that I miss her, and I'm frightened for her, and I want her back. I can't bear losing her, not after losing Ashley. It's just too cruel a thing. Too cruel."

Jon said, "When will you come home?"

"Not until I know something. I have to know what happened to her."

"And what if you never know?"

Constance pushed up again, and she was restless, and her left hand strayed to her neck, feeling the gold necklace she'd forgotten was there. "How can I go back to New York without her, to be alone? How can I face myself knowing I lost her? I was going to care for her, for God's sake, and I lost her."

"Constance, go easy on yourself," Jon consoled. "It wasn't your fault. Wherever Anne is, she's strong. We know that. Maybe she ran off because she wanted to begin again, and begin again on her own, with no one knowing her past or who she'd been or what had happened to her. She'll be okay, Constance, and I believe, with all my heart, that someday she *will* get in touch with you. If it's at all possible, she will get in touch. Of that, I'm certain."

CHAPTER 34
New York City 2008

L ate in the evening of December 22, 2008, Constance arrived in New York. She'd stayed in London for as long as was reasonable. Since the bomb blast, Anne had simply disappeared without a word, and there was no need to remain any longer.

Weary and defeated, Constance entered her New York apartment, followed by the stout doorman, Julio, who carried in her bags. She tipped and thanked him and, when he was gone, she left the bags in the hallway and moved into the living room.

Putting on the lights, she stood unmoving, listening to the quiet, staring at the wall clock. It was 11:24 p.m. She stared at the clock intensely, as if it held some secret code of meaning.

Her thoughts seemed weirdly silly and foreign to her, as if new wheels and gears had been installed in her head while she was in London. Was the time early, or was it late? Was time a fact or fiction? Was it a made-up thing, depending on where you were in the world?

They were five hours ahead in London. Three hours behind in L.A. In Australia? They were nearly a day ahead. So what was time anyway? Sometimes an hour is short, sometimes long, and one incident, late or early, can disrupt everything else around it. It can change a life forever.

Where was Anne? In what time?

A dizziness came over her. Constance shivered, then lowered onto the couch, peering down at her hands that were cupped in her lap. Loneliness seemed to blow across her like a cold wind, and she felt weak, deflated and helpless. Where was her usual strength and determination? Where was her iron will, her confidence that she could solve every problem and answer every challenging question?

Constance lifted her head and cast her eyes about the room. It didn't look familiar. Floor plants had been moved. The room's color scheme was wrong. There were accents of forest green, not the blue tones she'd chosen.

And where did that jade figurine of the goddess Guan Yin come from? Constance was familiar with Guan Yin, having traveled to China with her husband years ago. She was said to embody the totality of mercy, compassion, kindness and love. But where did the thing come from?

Constance churned with uneasiness and confusion. "You're exhausted," she said aloud, her voice rusty and low. "Go to bed."

With effort, she removed her makeup, showered, slipped into a cotton nightgown, tossed back the comforter and climbed into bed. In the bleak darkness, she wept, and she hadn't wept in a very long time.

CONSTANCE AWOKE THE NEXT MORNING to the distant sound of children; there was a squeal of laughter; footsteps outside her bedroom door. Sure she was still on the edge of a dream, she settled back down into the pillow, keeping her eyes tightly shut. It was a day she didn't want to face, even though sunlight was breaking through the half-closed, pleated, beige curtains.

A gentle knock on the door irritated her, and she ignored it. Another rap opened her eyes.

"Yes...?" she called, sharply.

"It's Clarisse, Mrs. Crowne."

"I don't want to be disturbed."

There was a pause, and then Clarisse said, "But they're here."

Constance pushed up on elbows. "Who's here?"

"The kids."

Constance sat up. "Kids? What kids? What on earth are you talking about?"

Clarisse's voice was meek. "Avery and Oliver are here, Mrs. Crowne."

Constance whispered hoarsely to herself. *What in the hell is going on?*

"Clarisse, who are Avery and Oliver?"

Another long pause. Constance again heard the spontaneous cries of children coming from what was surely the living room.

In a huff, Constance flung back the white comforter and swung her feet to the carpet, her feet finding her emerald slippers. She shouldered into her silk robe and padded to the door. Annoyed, she opened it, and Clarisse stood before her, contrite.

"You told me to tell you when they arrived, Mrs. Crowne."

Constance stared at her maid, searching her eyes. "Have you completely lost your mind?"

Clarisse stared down at the floor.

At that moment, a young, pretty woman, all smiles, appeared beside Clarisse.

Constance felt a hammer blow to her heart, and she nearly collapsed. She knew this woman. The face was older, yes, but she knew her! She was a mature woman in her early thirties, with sparkling eyes, rich black hair that rested on her thin shoulders, and a lovely, full mouth. Yes, she knew this woman.

Constance's pulse shot up. It was a lie. A lie of the eyes. A terrible and cruel lie. Her mind careened out of control, and she staggered.

The woman called out, concerned, reaching for her. "Mom, what's the matter?"

Constance felt herself go; felt every bit of muscle strength, mind strength, and spiritual strength rush out of her, and she wilted and dropped. Before losing consciousness, she heard Clarisse say, "Ashley, call 911. I think your mother has had a heart attack."

CONSTANCE AWOKE IN HER BED, hearing voices floating down to her. It was a woman's voice, and a man's voice. Her eyes fluttered open, and she saw Ashley and Jon Miles standing above her with strained, worried faces.

"Mom, how are you feeling?"

Constance stared at the woman. She tried to speak but failed.

Jon Miles said, "You gave us a scare, Constance. EMS came, and they were going to whisk you off to the ER, just as I got here. Your heart's fine. Pulse is good. Your blood pressure was a bit high, but its normal now. You just fainted."

Constance's head was pounding. "Fainted?" she said, weakly.

Jon said, "Yes, Constance. Now, as your son-in-law and sometimes doctor, I'm going to explain what fainting is. Fainting occurs when your brain temporarily doesn't receive enough blood supply, causing you to lose consciousness. The question is, why did your brain not receive enough blood supply? Ashley said that the second you saw her, your face went as white as paper. What happened?"

Constance couldn't pull her eyes from the woman, from Ashley, from her daughter, and the more she gazed at her, the more her mind tightened up.

"Mom... what happened?"

Ashley's voice seemed to come from far away. Constance forced out, "... Mom?"

Ashley took her mother's hand and kissed it. "Can I get you anything? I'll make you some breakfast. When was the last time you ate?"

"No... food..."

Jon cut in. "We need to talk about your medications, Constance. We can't have this happen again. The next time you fall, Ashley and Clarisse may not be there to catch you. You could seriously hurt yourself."

"Water?" Constance asked, and Ashley reached for the half-drunk glass on the night stand.

After Constance swallowed some, she handed the glass back to Ashley, her eyes never wavering from Ashley's face. Her eyes narrowed, then warmed, then searched again. "Ashley?"

"Yes, Mom... You're starting to worry me. Maybe you had a little stroke or something?"

Ashley glanced at Jon, anxiety rising in her. "Jon?"

Constance's eyes slid to Ashley and then back to Jon. "Jon... What was that you said?"

"I said, we may have to adjust your medications. Once you're up and around, let's make a list, and then call your real doctor."

Constance lifted a weak hand. "No... You said, son-in-law?"

Jon studied her, then nodded, suddenly concerned. "Yes, Constance... Okay, so maybe we need to get you to the hospital and run some tests."

"No... No... I'm fine. I'm... just..."

She was distracted by the low sounds of children's laughter outside. Her mind went into feverish thought. It leaped up and fell down; it searched the depths for reasons and connections. Had she had a stroke? No. Then what the hell happened? Was she hallucinating? Dreaming? Had she snapped and lost her mind? She kept hearing the word "time" tick in her head, like the swinging pendulum in a grandfather's clock. "Time. Time. Time. Time."

No, her mind was fine. She was fine. But something strange had happened. She'd sensed it the night before, when she'd seen the statue of Guan Yin and noticed the changed living room color scheme. But what? What had happened?

When the name Anne Billings shot into her head, she blinked rapidly, her brain lighting up, her face opening to something unthinkable. She felt suspended in space, and time melted away.

Constance worked to sit up, as all the flying pieces in her head began to coalesce into a new and stunning thought; a new and impossible reality. Her mind forced out ideas and theories, as she molded, arranged and rearranged the past and present into a brand-new thing— into a brand-new reality.

Ashley placed two pillows behind her mother's back, and Constance leaned back uncomfortably with a deep sigh.

"Bring me a Cognac," Constance said, her voice stronger.

"A Cognac? Mom? Are you sure?"

"I'm not sure that's a good idea," Jon said.

Constance gave him a stern glance. "Jon... Don't argue with me. Get me the damned Cognac."

Ashley and Jon traded glances of relief, as if to say, "She's all right. This is the Constance we know."

Jon smiled. "All right, Constance. I'll be right back."

Constance called after him. "Oh... Avery and Oliver..."

He turned back. "Yes?"

"My grandkids?"

Ashley lowered her eyes on her mother. "Mom... they're going crazy out there waiting to see you. They both bought you Christmas presents. I was going to put them under the tree, but there is no tree. What's going on? You always have a tree up two weeks before Christmas."

"Then go out and buy a tree," Constance demanded. "What are we waiting for? Go out and buy a tree this morning. Right now. Tell Jon. I'm ready to celebrate."

Ashley stepped back, her smile starting small, then growing. "Well, a Merry Christmas to you, too, Mom."

When the tears sprang to Constance's eyes, Ashley crouched down and took her hand.

"Everything is fine, Mom. You just fainted, but now you're fine. We're all here for Christmas, and I guarantee it will be the best Christmas of our lives."

EPLILOGUE
New York City 2008

Early the next morning, December 24, while Ashley slept in her old bedroom, Constance sat at the kitchen island sorting through stacks of mail. Although Jon and Ashley lived only fifteen blocks away, Ashley had stayed over to ensure her mother was alright. Jon and the kids had gone home the evening before but would return by early afternoon to celebrate Christmas Eve.

Constance and Ashley had talked late into the night and, for Constance, it had been the most joyful day of her life. She was still adjusting to her new reality—the golden reality of having her thirty-three-year-old daughter alive and happy, married to Dr. Jon Miles, with two lovely children.

Ashley had said, "When you introduced me to Jon, I knew he was Mr. Right. We just got along, and we still do. Even when we argue, most of the time we end up laughing or slipping off to the bedroom."

Constance kept her secret to herself—a secret that seemed tenuous and precious. She had few answers to the myriad of questions that this new reality had brought. She could only speculate, but not too much. Too much speculation might shatter the new heaven she was living in and send her crashing back to earth.

While Constance sipped coffee in the early morning light, her attention was drawn to an envelope near the middle of the pile. It wasn't a bill or junk mail. It stood out: it was a letter. Constance removed it from the stack and held it up. Her name and address were handwritten, in a neat and clean script. The return address read:

Claire Anne Edwards
2483 Edgecliff Road
Chicago, Ill 60076

Constance didn't open it right away. She couldn't. A feeling of dread crawled through her, a feeling that somehow the letter might smash her new and joyful life. The letter might reveal the truth, or a lie, or even worse, a joke. So she stared at it, her insides twisting.

After several sips of coffee and a bite of toast, Constance talked herself into opening the envelope, but she took her time, her shoulders stiff, her body tense, as if expecting a blow.

She drew the letter from the envelope with slow, anxious fingers. It was four pages, folded two times, handwritten. The first page's handwriting was distinctively different from the rest. Constance's eyes lingered over it; she swallowed, and then she read the first page.

Dear Mrs. Crowne:

My name is Claire Edwards, and I am Anne Billings Taylor's daughter. Before her death, my mother asked me to send you the following letter and ensure that it arrived after December 20, 2008. You will find my mother's letter enclosed.

My mother passed away in 1999, when she was eighty-one years old. In the last month of her life, she shared her fantastic story with me; the story of her time travel adventure from 1944 to 2008. She assured me she told no one else, including my father, who passed away in 1994. I will keep the secret as long as I live. Who would believe me anyway?

My mother wanted to live long enough to see you again and explain what happened but, as she said, "It wasn't meant to be."

My mother spoke of you often, with fondness, appreciation and love. The letter enclosed will perhaps be a helpful illumination for you.

I want to personally thank you for all you did for Mom. She was a great lady and a wonderful mother.

Yours sincerely,
Claire Edwards

Constance gazed sightlessly for a time, finally turning the first page over and reading the letter from Anne Billings.

Dearest Constance:

If you are reading this, then I have moved on to the next world of mystery. I wanted to live long enough to visit you in 2008, but it wasn't meant to be. I would have been ninety years old. Wouldn't that have been a reunion to celebrate, my dear friend?

The doctors tell me my heart is weak, as are other parts of the machinery, so I must write to you now while I am still strong enough, so I can tell you the rest of the story. Perhaps you know it, or most of it.

First, I want to say that without your determined and loving support, I would not have survived my time travel experience. I was as lost and forlorn as any orphan lamb, and so very confused, and so very troubled. But then you came into my life and unselfishly, with loving support, brought me back to life. I knew I could lean on you and trust you, and that got me through.

In London, when I ran from Reese Patrick's car, I felt a desperate sense of hopelessness. I couldn't think or feel. I just wanted to run. And run I did. When that young, earnest policeman told me about the bomb in Hyde Park, something in my head snapped, and it was as if I felt the call of—for lack of a better word—the call of destiny.

Like a mad woman, I ran toward Serpentine Lake, miraculously dodging the police, knowing full well that I might be about to meet my death. Still I ran, feeling a beckoning, an inexpressible urge to find that bomb.

When it went off, the force of the explosion tossed me into the air, and I lost consciousness. Upon awakening, I was in a London Hospital, crying out in pain and crying out for my son, Tommy. Miraculously and mysteriously, I had returned to 1944.

Days later, my mom and dad found me. Well, you can imagine how I felt. Completely and utterly confused, elated and very beaten up by the bomb blast.

Some days later, my Dad found Tommy at a separate hospital and, thank God, he'd not been fatally hurt. To boil it all down in a concise way, he and I survived the war, although it took some time for me to heal.

As luck would have it, Lieutenant Kenneth Taylor finished his ten missions, and he had to return home to the United States. He vowed he'd come back for me and, when the war was over, he did come back to England and we were married in 1946.

It took some months before we were able to leave for America with Tommy, but it all eventually worked out and I have spent my life in Chicago, married to a lovely man, a good and kind man. He became a lawyer and worked for his father's firm, eventually taking it over when his father died.

And are you ready for this, Constance? I had three wonderful children with Kenneth. I have been so blessed. Tommy returned to live in England after he finished college, and he married a nice girl there. They live in Cheltenham, a town in Gloucestershire, and Tommy is now retired and enjoying his three grandkids and working in his garden. I don't see him as often as I'd like, but he calls and writes regularly.

So you can see, Constance, that your kindness, generosity and support generated a wealth of happiness for many people.

I had to find some way to repay you, didn't I? I shall explain. Do you remember the night you told me about your daughter, Ashley's, terrible murder? You shared the day, the hour and the location of the event in Central Park. You even took me to the place where her body was found.

In March 1993, three days before Ashley was to be murdered, I traveled alone to New York, and booked a room in a hotel. I ventured by your building several times to "scope it out" as they say. I even saw you leave the building once and waited, while the doorman hailed you a cab. Seeing you there brought tears and a rush of warmth and love. Why didn't I show myself? I had a job to do, and I didn't want to chance it, playing with fate any more than I already had. There was another reason. As strange as it sounds, you wouldn't have known me. I didn't enter your life until October 2008. And there's more.

The day Ashley was to be murdered in Central Park, I was standing outside your building, waiting for her. It was a cold morning for that time of year and, believe you me, I was shivering when Ashley finally appeared in her jogging attire. Of course, I knew her from the photos you'd shown me in 2008.

When she emerged from the front door, I sprang into action, shuffling toward her, grimacing. I called out in pain just to make the scene even more dramatic. And then a strange thing happened that I cannot explain. When I reached out to Ashley and she turned to me, sparks shot out from my hand, and I felt a jolt of electricity shoot through my body as if I'd touched a live wire. Then I really did cry out in shock and pain.

Being concerned, Ashley approached. I watched, absolutely stunned, as she passed through a dancing, shimmering veil of blue light that seemed to separate us. For a few brief seconds, she and I were suspended in time and I could not move. Not one finger. And then the veil shattered, and Ashley and I shared the same space.

A moment later, Ashley was before me, and she asked, "Are you alright? Can I help you?"

I was genuinely frightened, and I did indeed feel my pulse racing and my heart pounding. I struggled to speak and said, "Oh, my. I believe it's my heart. Can you help me to the emergency room? I'm in great pain."

The doorman suddenly appeared, offering to help, but Ashley waved him away, saying she'd take care of me.

Well, Constance, your lovely daughter hailed a cab, helped me inside and traveled with me to the ER. She remained with me until I was examined and released.

Ashley didn't go jogging that day, Constance. She was with me at the time she would have been killed.

So, dear friend, you saved my life, and I saved Ashley's.

You may ask, "Why didn't you ever come to see me?"

Again, you would not have known me. I did not exist for you then. And it seems that for only the briefest moment in time, a couple of months in 2008, you and I lived in a different world from the world I helped to create by saving Ashley. I do not understand it, but I've had years to think about it, haven't I?

Perhaps when I saved Ashley from being killed, a separate world was born; a new world was born. When I reached for Ashley and those sparks shot out from my hand, perhaps I pierced a new world and another time. Maybe our two separate worlds somehow became connected, then merged, to form a new and different world. Can I say it? A better world, because Ashley was not murdered, and you did not have to suffer her loss.

Well, Constance, that's the best I can come up with. Of course, I have never told another soul about this. I suppose a physicist or psychic might have a different theory about it all, but I'm satisfied to know that Ashley is alive and well, and you and she will have a happy life together.

And so, my dear friend, enjoy your life with your lovely daughter, Ashley, and I will remember you in my thoughts and my prayers for as long as I live. You and I truly experienced something extraordinary but, ultimately, I became a better person; a more loving and grateful person, and for all I have been given, I am so thankful.

I hope you and your family are blessed with a full, rich and loving life. That is my daily prayer for you.

With deepest gratitude and love,
Anne Billings Taylor
September 29, 1998

Constance lifted her wet, blurring eyes from the page and stared ahead. Her emotions were running riot, and she couldn't stop the tears that spilled out and ran down her cheeks.

She carefully folded the letter and returned it to the envelope. Later, she'd place it in her home safe and keep it secret. Eventually, she'd burn the letter, but not now. Not until she'd read it a few more times. No one would believe the letter anyway, would they?

When Ashley wandered in, sleepy and hungry, Constance swiftly left her stool, reached for her daughter, and pulled her into a tight embrace.

"Well... good morning, Mom."

Ashley pulled back and held her mother at arm's length, searching her watering eyes. "Why are you crying? It's not like you. I can't remember the last time you cried."

Constance wiped the tears. "Can't a mother cry when she sees her daughter in the morning?"

Ashley smiled warmly. "Of course. It's just so sweet and, let's be honest, mother dear, you're not the most sentimental of women."

Constance snatched a tissue from the box on the counter and blotted her eyes. "So today, I'm sentimental. And, anyway, I was remembering an old friend."

"Anybody I know?"

Constance gave her a long look, and then thought better of reminding her daughter about the woman she'd taken to the ER fifteen years before.

"No, no one you know."

Constance turned and moved toward the coffee pot. "Want some coffee?"

"Please... Jon and the kids will be here soon. I'm going to need it."

After the coffee was poured, Constance went to the stove. "How about some eggs?"

"Will you have some?"

"Of course. Scrambled okay?"

"Perfect, with cheese and onion," Ashley said.

"I didn't know you liked onion in your scrambled eggs."

"Jon turned me on to it."

Constance nodded and went back to work. "By the way, did you give me that jade statue of Guan Yin?"

"You know I did. Three Christmases ago. Why do you ask?"

Constance shrugged. "No reason. I love it."

"So you said, when you opened the box."

Constance felt the tears come again, but she stopped them. She'd cried enough for one day. "You know, Ashley, I can't remember the last time we had breakfast together," knowing it was over fifteen years ago, at least as she remembered it.

"Well, you look much better this morning," Ashley said. "Your color is back, and you've got that determined look in your eyes again. You really had us worried."

Constance reached into the refrigerator for the carton of eggs and placed them next to a yellow bowl. As she cracked the eggs, Constance felt a quiet, rising joy spreading in her.

"Well, don't you worry about me anymore. I've never felt better in my life. Now sit down and let your mother make her daughter breakfast on Christmas Eve morning. I have so many things I want to ask you."

Thank You!

Thank you for taking the time to read *Time Stranger*. If you enjoyed it, please consider telling your friends or posting a short review. Word of mouth is an author's best friend, and it is much appreciated.

Thank you,
Elyse Douglas

The Christmas Diary
The Christmas Diary – Book 2 - Lost and Found
Christmas for Juliet
The Christmas Bridge
The Date Before Christmas
The Christmas Women
Christmas Ever After
The Summer Diary
The Summer Letters
The Other Side of Summer
Wanting Rita

Time Travel Novels
The Christmas Eve Letter (A Time Travel Novel) Book 1
The Christmas Eve Daughter (A Time Travel Novel) Book 2

The Christmas Eve Secret (A Time Travel Novel) Book 3
The Christmas Eve Promise (A Time Travel Novel) Book 4
The Lost Mata Hari Ring (A Time Travel Novel)
The Christmas Town (A Time Travel Novel)
Time Change (A Time Travel Novel)
Time Shutter (A Time Travel Novel)
Time Sensitive (A Time Travel Novel)

Romantic Suspense Novels
Daring Summer
Frantic
Betrayed

www.elysedouglas.com

Editorial Reviews

THE LOST MATA HARI RING – A Time Travel Novel
by Elyse Douglas

"This book is hard to put down! It is pitch-perfect and hits all the right notes. It is the best book I have read in a while!"
5 Stars!
--Bound4Escape Blog and Reviews

"The characters are well defined, and the scenes easily visualized. It is a poignant, bitter-sweet emotionally charged read."

5-Stars!
--Rockin' Book Reviews

"This book captivated me to the end!"
--StoryBook Reviews

"A captivating adventure..."
--Community Bookstop

"...Putting *The Lost Mata Hari Ring* down for any length of time proved to be impossible."
--Lisa's Writopia

"I found myself drawn into the story and holding my breath to see what would happen next..."
--Blog: A Room Without Books is Empty

Editorial Reviews

THE CHRISTMAS TOWN – A Time Travel Novel
by Elyse Douglas

"The Christmas Town is a beautifully written story. It draws you in from the first page, and fully engages you up until the very last. The story is funny, happy, and magical. The characters are all likable and very well-rounded. This is a great book to read during the holiday season, and a delightful read during any time of the year."
--Bauman Book Reviews

"I would love to see this book become another one of those beloved Christmas film traditions, to be treasured over the years! The characters are loveable; the settings vivid. Period details are believable. A delightful read at any time of year! Don't miss this novel!"
--A Night's Dream of Books

THE SUMMER LETTERS – A Novel
by Elyse Douglas

"A perfect summer read!"
--Fiction Addiction

"In Elyse Douglas' novel THE SUMMER LETTERS, the characters' emotions, their drives, passions and memories are all so expertly woven; we get a taste of what life was like for veterans, women, small town folk, and all those people we think have lived too long to remember (but they never really forget, do they?).
I couldn't stop reading, not for a moment. Such an amazing read. Flawless."
5 Stars!
--Anteria Writes Blog - To Dream, To Write, To Live

"A wonderful, beautiful love story that I absolutely enjoyed reading."
5 Stars!
--Books, Dreams, Life - Blog

"The Summer Letters is a fabulous choice for the beach or cottage this year, so you can live and breathe the same feelings and smells as the characters in this wonderful story."
--Reads & Reels Blog

Printed in Great Britain
by Amazon